UNANSWERED PRAYERS

"So, why did you and your husband break up?" Sam leaned toward her as he softly asked the question.

"It's the same old story, nothing you'd be interested in." Naomi did not want to talk about her ex-husband with Sam. It would give him too much information.

"I'll bet it's *not* the same old story. I can't figure it out. It couldn't have been that you were fooling around—you're too decent for that. You're smart and funny and caring and beautiful. After last night, I know it couldn't have been the sex, so what was it?"

"It *was* the sex." *Why did I blurt that out?* She hoped he could not see her flaming cheeks in the half-light of the stage.

"That's not funny." Sam looked up at her face. "You mean it, it really was the sex?"

MORGAN MALONE

Unanswered PRAYERS

DEDICATION

For Garth Brooks.

I grew up in the country but never liked country music until I heard "That Summer" late one night while driving my daughter home from high school. Thank you for opening up a wonderful world of music and words for me. And thank you for the best concert ever in Buffalo 2015. In my writer's soul, you are Sam.

And for MLH, always.

ACKNOWLEDGEMENTS

While most of the characters in this book are fictional, some of them are real people. Obviously, none of the celebrities mentioned ever toured with Sam Rhodes or recorded any songs with him and his band. I included the performers who I would have loved to see on this "dream" tour. I hope they take no offense at my portrayal of them as I love and respect them and their music. The song, "In Another's Eyes", was in fact recorded by Garth Brooks and Trisha Yearwood. It was, however, not written by Sam Rhodes, but beautifully created by Garth Brooks, Bobby Wood and John Peppard.

I would like to thank Sean and Ritchie, co-hosts of the Morning Show on WGNA, 107.7 FM, Albany, NY for all the great Country Music that woke me up after long nights working on this book. It was their voices that, in fact, first informed me of the events of 9/11.

Thank you to LuAnn McLane, author extraordinaire, friend, mentor, drinking buddy and an invaluable source of advice and support for "my" country singer story.

My thanks to my writing group, Writing Women's Minds (Maggie, Posey, Sharon and Jean), for their encouragement and constructive criticism. Many thanks also to my two Beta-Readers, Sue G. and Sue W., for catching my grammatical mistakes, my plotting errors and for correcting my Yiddish.

And to my editor, Deelylah Mullin, my profound gratitude for taking a story I could only imagine thirteen years ago and helping me turn it into the book I always hoped it would be.

TABLE OF CONTENTS

PROLOGUE—2016

She paused in front of the floor-to-ceiling windows, wrapped only in a towel. The Manhattan skyline never failed to give her pause. Especially when viewed from her penthouse suite. Even when she knew it would delay her timely arrival at the American Music Awards for a few more minutes, and she was already risking a strong scolding for her tardiness. *So what?* This was a once in a lifetime night, and she was going to savor every second of the experience.

A glittering black gown hung from the open closet door; its silk and sequins fell in a cascade from the tiny strapless top through the full sweep of the skirt. *God bless Marchesa.* Jimmy Choo black silk sandals sat beneath it on the plush carpet. Ruby and pearl clusters were already sparkling in her ears, and the rest of the Harry Winston suite of red and cream lay on the dresser.

She stood in front of the windows, watching the city lights blink on in the gathering dusk. Time stood still as memories swept over her. She shivered, not from the draft on her bare legs, but from a tumbled mix of emotion. The aching emptiness from the absence of the Twin Towers, the energetic hum from the street noises far below, the neon flash of the marquees, and the acute awareness of how close she had come to losing all of this.

Had it really been fifteen years ago that her journey to this place had begun? Manhattan had been the catalyst, then as now, for all her great adventures. And what a roller-coaster ride had begun on that hot summer day just a few blocks away from where she now stood.

CHAPTER ONE—2001

"I will be *God-damned* if I am going to spend my summer *schlepping* around the Mid-west in a bus with a bunch of *yahoos!*" Naomi Stein flung her long curls over her shoulder as she stomped away from Jed's wide mahogany desk. She stood in front of his expansive view of Manhattan, fuming at the unfairness of the Special Features Editor's suggestion. "I don't *do* country music. You know that!" she spat at him, accusingly.

Jedediah Weiss leaned back in his leather chair, arms folded across his broad chest, waiting and watching Naomi. The two of them had known each other since their days at Cornell. Jed had often commented Naomi should be performing on the stage herself instead of writing about it. Naomi knew she was working herself into a fine state, which, she had been told, was always a sight.

"Now, Naomi," Jed began.

"Don't 'now Naomi' me!" She snarled as she whirled back to face him. She pushed her hair off her face and her eyes narrowed. Slamming her hands onto Jed's desk, the angry reporter got in his face.

"*Now, Jed,*" she said through clenched teeth, "you listen to me. You promised me six weeks off this summer, and I planned my summer around that promise. Jonah will be at camp for four weeks, and then he is going to David's for two weeks. I am going to the Cape for a month to *veg out*. Then, I am heading up north for some more peace and quiet while I edit my book. A trip through middle America on a tour bus is not on my agenda and is not going to be!"

"Naomi, Sam Rhodes is the hottest entertainment story of the year. You should be kissing me for getting you in on his tour instead of screaming at me like a *vilde chai*! This is a huge story, and you are the only one to write it. You have done a great job with the country music acts you've covered for us. Remember Farm Aid? How many years did you *schlepp* around with Willie Nelson? Besides, I've even persuaded your favorite photographer, William, to give you two weeks for the photographs. *He's* postponing a trip to Morocco for you. Besides, with Jonah in camp, you'll have no scheduling hassles. And the last time you went to the Cape, you came back with sun poisoning—you were sick for a week!"

That Jed was right didn't make it any easier to swallow. She knew more than a little about the country scene—how could you write about the music industry and not write about country? It had seen such a huge increase in popularity in the 1990s, thanks to Garth Brooks and others. She had even written about Garth on more than one occasion.

But Naomi was at the stage in her career—her hard-fought for career—when she could almost always choose the subject matter of her assignments. Her uncanny ability to get inside what was *hot* in the music industry had played no small part in her rise to the top, with her articles frequently earning the cover of *Rolling Stone*, *Entertainment Weekly*, *Vogue*, and *GQ*. She got close to her subjects—she had that *Earth Mother* persona that drew people to her and made them feel comfortable letting their hair down. And, she could write, really write.

Naomi was in the process of editing the copy to accompany a series of rock star portraits photographed by Annie Liebovitz, soon to be published as *the* season's coffee table book. All she needed was some uninterrupted quality time to glean suitable pieces from her years of reporting, and write some updates. With her twelve-year old son, Jonah, ensconced—albeit unwillingly—in Sunrise Lake Camp in the Catskills, she wanted nothing more than a cottage on Cape Cod to relax and write. At thirty-six, Naomi felt more like eighty-six. Years of non-stop reporting for *Rolling Stone* and other magazines had worn her out. She might have been able to rally, but the constant battles in the past year with Jonah and his passive-aggressive father, her ex-husband David, left her frazzled and frustrated. She needed a break from the men in her life; she needed a break from men telling her what to do, even if the man was Jed.

And now her *dear* friend Jed was shipping her off to Texas!

"Jed, why do I have to go on tour with him? I could go to a few concerts before I leave for the Cape, interview the band and Sam Rhodes, then have an article for you in a couple of weeks. I don't need to *tour* with him, for God's sake. I haven't been on tour with anyone in two years—and that was Elton John!"

"Honey, you know you have to go out on the road with him. Sam's doing something completely different, and it's so damn exciting even *you* can't capture it in a few shows! You have to go. You know who opened the tour with him? Tina! I'll bet even Springsteen is gonna show on this tour!"

Sam Rhodes. All Naomi had been hearing about lately was Sam Rhodes. Sure, he'd had a long career in country music—close to twenty years—but talk about his new album and this tour was on everyone's lips. She folded her arms across her chest and stuck out her lower lip in a full-fledged pout. She knew she was famous for that sulk. "Didn't he retire or something? What's with this album anyway? I know everybody loves him, or says they love him, but I don't really get all the excitement."

Jed was raking his fingers through his thick black hair obviously frustrated with her. "Are you serious? After three years hiding out in the Rockies, he reemerges with an album that goes platinum almost immediately. An album of everyone else's songs, all the songs that inspired him to become a musician, to become a songwriter; and all the songs that helped him find himself again. And he's got the biggest names in rock and country singing with him on the album *and* showing up on tour!"

It's true, Naomi mused. *Everyone was practically clambering to work with him. No one had a bad thing to say about Sam Rhodes, not even his ex-wives. What was his gimmick?* Her curiosity was piqued; she was starting to warm to the idea.

"Well," she said, "how is this going to work? If I go, I mean. Did he ask for me?"

"We asked him if we could send a writer and a photographer out on tour with him and his people okay'd it. Of course, your name *was* mentioned. I guess he really liked the article you did last year on B.B. King."

That *had* been one of her best articles, and it was to be included in the Liebovitz book. Against her will, Naomi was becoming intrigued with the notion of touring with a band again. And these were *good ole country boys*—there probably wouldn't be nearly the amount of drugs, sex and alcohol she had come across in prior years, following rock stars across the country. At thirty-six, she was slowing down a bit from her early days at *Rolling Stone*, when she was grateful just to have a job, when she went for coffee, proof-read other writers' articles, and was Jed's assistant's assistant.

Naomi started at the bottom at twenty-seven, with a toddler and a third-floor walk-up apartment in the Village. After putting David—the blood-sucking lawyer—through law school and scrimping while he worked for slave wages as an associate, Naomi found herself left alone with a toddler to raise when her husband dumped her as soon as he made senior associate at Ruthman Miller. The divorce was ugly, but Naomi fought him for Jonah's sake. She hadn't touched a dime of the settlement money she finally wrested from her ex-husband. All the money was in trust for Jonah—for college, a trip to Europe, a sports car, graduate school—whatever he wanted, within reason, of course. She was not a Jewish mother for nothing. That of course did not mean she wasn't making David pay child support, adjusted every time he got a promotion at Ruthman Miller. The law firm and a young brunette associate had taken her son's father away from him; they might as well compensate him for the loss, although it had turned out to be no great loss. David was such a *schmuck*!

Yeah, those early years had been lean and mean. Naomi took every assignment offered, toured the country a dozen times with upcoming stars, stars on the way down, stars with problems, and stars with gifts. Rock bands and girl groups, divas and super-star legends, she wrote about them all. And made a respected name for herself and a good life for her and her son.

"All right," she sighed. "I'll go. *Only* if I can have William, a new laptop computer with a DVD player, *and* the cover."

"Done!" Jed exclaimed. "I know better than to haggle with you. You learned from a pro, your Jewish mother, about haggling. I know I will end up losing even more if I start trying to make deals with you, my old friend! I think this will be great for you and for the magazine. Hell, I'll even give you a manicurist, masseuse, and your own cook, if that is what it would take to get your tush on the plane to Texas in two days." Naomi felt heat creep across her cheeks at his words. He had been so good to her in the past, she was not going to make him suffer any more—though she wished he could find someone to pack for her. They hugged before she left his office. She was getting excited about the project. *If anyone could pry the secrets of the last three years out of Sam Rhodes, it is me. Jed always says I can wrangle a story out of a stone.*

I need a massage, no, I need a wife, Naomi thought the next day as she juggled unpacking for the Cape and packing for a tour—somehow she knew she wouldn't need three swimsuits on this road trip—giving details of her trip to her personal assistant, Janice, and notifying Jonah's camp about her changed itinerary. *I cannot believe I gave in to Jed's bribery so easily. What am I going to do with my book, with Jonah, and when am I going to get a break? I am so close to burnout. I have been promising myself a vacation since January. And Jonah is being such a pain in my tush.* Three angry calls from camp to complain and the slamming of the phone reverberating in her ear was the result when she told him she was going to be touring with Sam Rhodes.

"Some *putz* gets your attention, and I'm stuck up here in the woods because you don't have enough time for me? Thanks a lot, Mom. Guess I know where your priorities are," Jonah retorted.

"Jonah, listen," she pleaded, "It doesn't make any difference where I am. You always go to Sunrise Lake in July. You didn't want to come home last year, remember?"

"Well, it's not last year, is it? I'm too old for camp. I want to hang with my friends. Why can't I stay with Dad?" He slammed the phone down so hard she was sure the camp was going to bill her for damages.

Naomi did not have the heart to tell him his father didn't want him; it was difficult enough to get the bloodsucker to take him for two weeks in August and a few weekends during the year.

With a new trophy wife and a new family to occupy his time, David did not want the hassles associated with an adolescent. It wasn't that Naomi wanted to let Jonah go with David, but she was determined that he have quality time with his father, that *he* never feel unwanted by a parent. *Been there, done that.* Jonah's frustrations with his father's evasions and cancellations always fell on Naomi. The battle about camp arose when David mentioned in passing at Passover that he, Courtney, and the new baby were going to be in the Hamptons in July and maybe Jonah could spend the month with them. Jonah took it as a *fait accompli.* When David later reneged, offering only two weeks in the city in August, Jonah, of course, blamed Naomi. *Classic. Why is it the absent father always smells like a rose and the mom gets all the shit? Who said you can have it all? Must have been some guy!*

She finally finished packing around one in the morning. The loft was clean, the mail directed to her office, and the newspaper delivery stopped. Naomi was nothing if not organized. A call was in for a car to take her to Kennedy for her early bird flight the next morning, and she had baked a double batch of chocolate chip cookies, one packed and mailed to Jonah, and one for William. William dearly loved her chocolate chip cookies, and as Naomi switched off the Tiffany lamp on her nightstand and turned to stare up at the New York City night through her skylight, she just knew she was going to need someone on her side when she met the enigmatic Mr. Rhodes.

CHAPTER TWO

"Hoss, you won't believe what just walked in," Tyrone whispered in his deep, raspy voice.

Sam looked up from the acoustic guitar he had been idly strumming. He glanced at Tyrone's grizzled face and followed the direction of his raised eyebrow to the aisle that ran down the center of American Airlines Center, bisecting the crowded rows of folding chairs.

"Well, I'll be *damned*," he swore and then let out a low whistle. Stalking down the aisle was Naomi. Followed by a photographer loaded with cameras, followed by Sam's band members Beau and Mickey, both grinning widely, cowboy hats pushed back on their heads.

"That is New York. Boy, that is *New York City!*" Sam exclaimed. He turned his faded University of Oklahoma baseball cap around, bill to the back, and leaned forward for a better look. His blue eyes swept over Naomi, head to foot and back again. He shook his head and whistled long and low again. Surprising himself, he realized he liked what he saw; he liked it a lot. All that wild, curly blonde hair, swinging around her shoulders, pushed back from a face that was not so much attractive as it was arresting, by the black Ray-Ban sunglasses that acted as a headband. Long shapely legs encased in faded black denim. The huge black leather bag, slung from her shoulder and resting on her hip, pulled the black leather blazer back from a truly remarkable chest.

Those are real, he thought and smiled in sincere appreciation at the way her breasts moved under the white T-shirt. She was at the steps to the stage now, and as she climbed up, he saw her boots.

Her red leather cowboy boots, faded from years of wear.

"I will be God-damned, boy, look at those boots. Whoo-eee!" he nudged Tyrone.

He looked over at Tyrone to see if he, too, had been appreciating Naomi's purposeful stride and everything that went with it. But Tyrone was not looking at Naomi. His gaze was fixed on Sam. Sam saw a look of concern pass over the older man's face.

"It's gonna be a long, hot summer," Tyrone muttered aloud, as both he and Sam rose and snatched off their hats.

"Damned if these two aren't *good ole boys*, just like I predicted," Naomi turned and muttered softly to William before she moved across the stage to extend her hand first to Tyrone. "Mr. Butler, it is so nice to see you again. We met at Farm Aid '96, remember?"

"Well, yes, missy, now I remember," Tyrone drawled. "You were following Neil Young around that night. I don't recollect that ole Neil was being very cooperative, though."

A blush rose on her cheeks "That interview was a real bitch." Naomi paused for a moment, as her face fell. "Not one of my best pieces; Neil definitely wasn't forthcoming. Still isn't."

She laughed, a deep, throaty sound that hit Sam in his gut like a shot of Sammy Hagar's tequila. Her face lit up with self-deprecating humor, the brown of her eyes warming to the color of bourbon.

"Let's just say, Mr. Butler, that I'm not one of his favorite journalists and his work is no longer included in my CD collection."

Tyrone laughed too, slapping his straw cowboy hat against his thigh. "Little girl, you've got some grit, for sure." He gestured toward Sam. "Honey, don't you worry none about that happening with Sam here. He's just naturally talkative, and he's as easy as an ole shoe to get around!"

Sam glared at Tyrone, as Naomi turned toward him, extending her hand.

"Mr. Rhodes, it's a pleasure to meet you," she said, raising an eyebrow. Sam knew he was scowling at her. She made him feel uncomfortable and damned if he knew why. Her slim hand with its bright red fingertips disappeared into his big calloused hand. Her touch felt cool in his warm grasp, cool and strong. He looked down at her curious eyes, lightening under his gaze from brown to almost gold. He towered over her, his six foot three inches big-boned frame at least a foot taller than Naomi. She was short, but not tiny. Her figure was lush and filled out her jeans and T-shirt in a way that made him scowl even more. And made him hard. *Damn.*

"Ma'am," was all Sam managed, as he finally released her hand. *Lord, the woman is something. She looks like she could chew me up and spit me out if I even thought about stepping out of line.* He knew she could write; he and everyone else had read her articles about the various singers and bands that streaked across the charts for the better part of the past decade. She was direct, without being nasty; incisive, without being exploitative; and honest. He knew just about everyone from LA to Boston who played a guitar or wrote songs or sang and every article she wrote about performers and songwriters, artists and producers, had rung true for Sam. *But I did not know how stunning, no, compelling, her face is.*

What am I going to do with her? He didn't much care for the notion she was going to splash his private life across the pages of *Rolling Stone*. He was *country*, and he did not want any of his old friends or loyal fans thinking he was crossing over for the money. Sam really could not figure out why the press, the fans, and the industry were all making such a fuss about this summer's tour. Country stars had been singing rock songs for decades, in their own special way. Just because some of the rock stars had joined him on the album when he was covering their songs and had agreed to come out on the tour, wasn't such a big deal. But Tommy, his oldest friend and road manager, got the idea they would not announce in advance who was going to be with them. That had lent the tour a certain cachet. And it allowed for last minute changes when schedules and travel plans got fouled up. His long-time guitarist and his drummer, Beau and Mickey, had played on the album with him so they knew the songs, and Tyrone had masterminded the idea in the first place, to help lift him out of the depression he had sunk into after the accident. Bobbi and JoEllen could sing backup with anyone, at almost a moment's notice, and they had sung the duets of the female stars on the demo tapes. It was pure show business, for sure, but it was a great hit with his fans. And Sam was only too painfully aware how much he owed to his fans. Roused from his thoughts by Naomi's red nails tapping on her purse, Sam faced the feisty reporter.

"If you'll just see Tommy over there, he'll fix you up with backstage passes and the like for you and your photographer," Sam said, nodding to William, who was already snapping away. "You're staying at the Hilton with us, I guess, on the same floor or nearby. We're just getting a sound check underway, if you want to watch, or someone can take you to the hotel to freshen up or rest…or whatever." He just wanted to put some distance between himself and this blonde with the New York City attitude, inquiring eyes, and tempting body.

"Thank you, Mr. Rhodes, but I'll just hang around here, if you don't mind. Who's the mystery guest tonight?" Naomi's face remained impassive, her voice cool.

"Kenny Rogers is stopping by, I believe. He's in Branson, so he's just flying over for the night. He should be here directly. Do you know him? I expect he hasn't been featured in *Rolling Stone* lately." Sam snickered.

"Actually, I write for other magazines on occasion. I've met Mr. Rogers before, Mr. Rhodes." Sam saw the color creeping up on Naomi's impressive cheekbones and found himself wondering if everything he said to her all summer was going to piss her off. The thought amused him, and he deepened his drawl just to watch her reaction.

"Please, call me Sam. We're going to be bumping into each other a lot in the next weeks and we don't stand on ceremony around here, Miss, er, Naomi."

He pronounced it *Nay-o-me*, like Naomi Judd.

"It's *Ni-o-me*, Mr. Rhodes, I mean, Sam," she corrected him. "It's the Biblical pronunciation."

Out of the corner of his eye, Sam could see Tyrone grinning at the exchange. Naomi had her back up about something, and she was really starting to grate on his nerves. *Yup, this is going to be one damn interesting tour.*

She knows her stuff. Sam watched Naomi covertly through the sound check, as she walked around the arena and the backstage area, talking with the crew and the rest of the band. Mickey and Beau had obviously fallen under her spell on the ride in from the airport, and she was making fast friends with Bobbi, his cousin.

Only his mercurial lead guitarist, Chase, was being a bit gun-shy, and JoEllen had not even glanced Naomi's way once.

He is gorgeous. And it was a surprise to her. Naomi could not think why she had never noticed Sam's before—he was big all over, or at least what she could see, not lanky, but big-boned and hard. Certainly, his music was not her style, and she only infrequently wrote about country artists, but she had been around Nashville, Atlanta and, of course, LA and New York. He had performed at some of the benefit concerts she'd covered, but she never really noticed his looks or his music. *But he is awfully full of himself or something.* Naomi couldn't put her finger on it.

Sam was strumming his old acoustic guitar, bending toward Tyrone as they discussed some detail of the song he was playing. She turned to signal William to get the shot, but he was already there, clicking away. William winked at her and tossed his dread locks out of his face, switching to the other camera that hung around his neck. He saw her watching Sam intently and grinned impudently.

"You'd think I never looked at an artist before," she huffed inwardly.

"Hello, gorgeous," someone chuckled in her ear. Well, she knew *that* voice. It was like honey and whiskey mixed together. And it belonged to just one person.

"Hi there, stranger." Naomi smiled widely as she reached around the broad shoulders of Kenny Rogers to give him a bear hug. She ran one hand up into his perfectly groomed white hair. "You still have the softest hair of any man I ever knew. Why haven't I ever run off with you? You've asked me enough times."

"Don't rub it in, Naomi. It is one of my greatest embarrassments that I have never been able to convince you that I am the answer to your prayers. But then, a sweet young thing like you doesn't need to hook up with an old reprobate like me." Those beautiful eyes sparkled at her as Kenny held her in a warm embrace. They met years before on Long Island when she worked for *Newsday*. She had been pregnant for Jonah, and he had taken pity on the young reporter with the swollen ankles who came looking for an interview while he was appearing at Westbury. Kenny had talked about his young son and forever charmed Naomi with his humor and empathy. He ended up rubbing her ankles for her and gave her one of the best interviews she had done up to that point in her fledgling career. Or since.

"Honey, we both know you're only interested in *sweet, young things*. I'm actually much too old for you." She teased him. Kenny laughed out loud, loud enough to have Sam's head whip around toward the sound. Naomi saw the smile that had started to spread across his hard features—like an isolated mountain, craggy, wind-burned and…cold—disappear when he saw Kenny's arms draped around her.

Kenny whispered into Naomi's ear before he let her loose. She giggled and gave him a loud kiss before he strode across the stage to greet Sam. Sam's ears were turning red as the country superstar approached, but he stretched his hand out to Kenny.

"Good to see you. I thought you might not make it, with all the weather, but I'm glad you did. Do you two…uh…know each other?" Sam nodded toward Naomi.

Kenny seemed a little taken aback by the tone of Sam's question. Naomi saw him look over at Tyrone, who shrugged in answer to Kenny's quizzical look. *Something was definitely cooking up here. What is the problem with these boys?*

"I was her first…no, second, interview a long, long time ago. I'm surprised she even remembers me, given the illustrious personages she's interviewed since." He laughed.

"Yes, you're definitely forgettable compared to Milli Vanilli and…" Naomi trailed off, laughing.

"Well, she's certainly slumming now," Sam retorted, none too kindly.

"Do you mean you or me, Hoss?" Tyrone called out. It broke the tension of the moment.

After a few minutes of good-natured ribbing, the musicians settled down to rehearse. Naomi once again faded into the background as Sam, Kenny and Tyrone worked through the set Kenny would do that evening.

Later that night, ensconced in her hotel room, wishing Kenny had not headed back to Missouri so he could rub her feet, Naomi reflected on what she had witnessed at the concert. *Jed was right*, though she was not going to admit it to him—at least not for the time being. Screaming, devoted fans packed the arena—that was nothing new to her. But, there had been something more. When Sam took the stage—promptly at eight o'clock, which was in itself virtually unheard of in her experience—there was a deafening roar. He stood in the center of the stage, cradling his old wreck of a guitar, a single spot on him, bleaching his faded T-shirt and jeans to almost pure white, with a small, sad smile playing around his lips. The crowd quieted to almost a breathless, silent anticipation.

Sam sang "Yesterday" accompanied by nothing but his guitar and Bobbi on the piano. Naomi was sure there was a tear in his eye. The crowd was almost motionless, watching him. When he finished, there was no outburst of applause, no screams, but, silence. Then the audience raised their arms almost as one, holding lighters and matches throughout the darkened arena. It seemed to go on for minutes, though surely it had only been a few seconds before the huge gathering erupted. She thought him crazy, opening with a slow song, but he held the audience in the palm of his hand, from the very beginning. She had seen that kind of possession only once before: Eric Clapton. And, *Clapton is God*!

Later, when Sam strummed the opening chords of "Lady", the audience gave him the expected reaction as the second spot played over to Kenny, just left of center stage. The two did a sweet job with the song, and their between-song banter was evidence of the respect and affection they had for each other. Sam then joked with Kenny about what other song they could sing together, and Kenny replied he was partial to "We've Got Tonight." That had brought a huge laugh from the audience as Sam queried whether he was to sing Kenny's or Sheena Easton's part. They decided they would sing Kenny's part together and leave Sheena's to Bobbi and JoEllen. But no one could have predicted the reaction when it was not Sam's back-up singers who stepped up to the mic, behind and to the right of Sam and Kenny, but Stevie Nicks. It was pure show business. Even Sam was surprised. *That* had been Kenny's whispered secret to Naomi.

Still smiling from the scene she had witnessed, Naomi rose from the desk where she was checking her email and took a bottle of spring water from the small fridge in her room. Comfy in her favorite old nightshirt, she walked around in her bare feet, arching her back trying to loosen muscles that had tightened during her first long day on Sam's tour. *I'm getting too old for this crap.* She smiled at her reflection in the night-darkened window. Sam's jaw had dropped about a foot when he realized that it was Stevie singing. He had stood almost dumbfounded while Kenny had a good laugh and the audience roared. Then Naomi frowned as she remembered the way Sam lifted Stevie in his arms at the song's end. The kiss he gave her was way beyond friendly to Naomi's way of thinking. *Well, that's his business.* Still, she could not deny their duet on "Leather and Lace" was better than the original. *I wonder if those two ever had anything going on?* Stevie left almost immediately after the show; Naomi had just gotten a few words with the elusive singer and had no time to really question her.

Well, I hope William got pictures of all of it. Of course he had. William Blake was the best concert photographer in the business. They started out at the same time and throughout the 1990s found themselves often covering the same shows. A lasting friendship formed between the young journalist and the untried photographer, as they battled the inherent prejudices against a Jewish woman and an African-American man. After the show, William promised to stay with her through the end of the month. *Bless him. I'm going to have to find a Mrs. Fields to keep him happy.* When Naomi's chocolate chip cookies were not available, William grudgingly settled for Mrs. Fields.

And she needed William so she had at least one player on her team. Naomi felt alone in the midst of Sam's enormous entourage. Sam's band and crew formed an almost solid wall around him; they performed as though they could read each other's minds. Most of them had been with Sam since the start of his career. She had her work cut out for her if she wanted to pry some personal information about him from them. God knew she probably would not get too much out of Sam himself. Naomi snorted: *Easy as an ole shoe, my ass*!

CHAPTER THREE

They left Dallas for Oklahoma City the next morning. Sam and the band traveled in two luxurious tour buses, the crew in two nicely equipped buses, followed by a caravan of tractor-trailers hauling instruments, rigging, lights, catering equipment, luggage and who knew what else. Sam's road manager and best friend, Tommy Beckett, eschewed the buses, tooling along in the black Lincoln Navigator that had been a gift from Sam, chattering into his speakerphone, and juggling all the insanity that went with being the tour manager. As this was her first day out, Naomi made a point of riding in the bus that was *not* carrying Sam. Something about him still annoyed her, and she could not quite place what it was. And he certainly was *not* thrilled with her. She had fired a blistering e-mail off to Jed. *Sam had asked for her. Right!* Her *old* friend Jedediah Weiss would be paying big time for this escapade.

She boarded the bus wearing her trademark black denims, white T-shirt, and the worn red boots she had bought years ago at a riding shop near Saratoga Springs with her first big paycheck from *Rolling Stone.* It had been the first time every penny she earned had not been earmarked for bills or Jonah's savings. The boots never failed to bolster her spirits, and she definitely needed the boost.

She settled in with Bobbi and JoEllen. Naomi found the women who traveled with bands or who were members of bands often had the best insights into the dynamics of the group and the star. Naomi knew the basic details of Sam's story: three wives, two divorces, and then the death of his third wife and little girl while he was finishing up his last tour. She had heard of his descent into grief, accompanied by endless bottles of tequila. Two, maybe three, years ago. She suspected it had been Tyrone who brought Sam back to life. Tyrone had been with Sam for almost twenty years, leaving his own established career to play guitar with the upstart from Oklahoma.

As the bus moved from Texas to Sam's home state, Naomi quickly realized neither woman had a negative comment to make about Sam. Naomi hadn't expected too much from Bobbi Gardner, who was, after all, Sam's cousin. Bobbi had been with him almost from the first and was extremely loyal. Not that she couldn't see Sam as he was, Bobbi told Naomi.

"But he's had it rough, and if he slipped a few times, well, he always found his way back, didn't he?" Bobbi paused to take a sip from her ever-present bottle of water.

"My Uncle Frank—he was married to my mom's sister, Suzie—he was a hard man. He was an athlete, played some semi-pro ball before he got drafted into the Army. Uncle Frank stayed in for two tours, and when he came back, he started working construction in my grandfather's company. He met Aunt Suzie there; he was older than her. She and my mother are both registered nurses. Did you know that? Well, Aunt Suzie married Uncle Frank, and they settled down and had Sam." Bobbi sighed and then leaned toward Naomi as she continued.

"My uncle was always rough on Sam—wanted him to be tough, wanted him to measure up. Sam could never do that because Uncle Frank kept moving the bar higher and higher. Sam got an A, why wasn't it an A-plus? Sam made the football team, why wasn't he the captain? You know what I mean?"

Naomi nodded her head. She knew exactly what Bobbi meant. Her own father had wanted a son. He got two daughters—her older sister Miriam and her. He was happy enough about Miriam, who looked just like his mother, he often said, and who carried that tragic figure's name. But he had expected Naomi to be a boy. He was never quite able to hide his disappointment in her. Naomi, too, never quite measured up. In a household of women, Alex Stein's word had been law, and his every whim catered to by her mother, Lilli, and her sister. In order to get any attention from her forbidding father, Naomi resorted to acting out and acting up. That made life at home even more difficult for the hurt and lonely girl.

"Sam wanted to sing in the church choir with his mom; he loved singing even when he was little boy. His father didn't dare forbid him because Aunt Suzie and my mom Charlene loved singing in church. I think Sam and I got our voices from our moms. But Uncle Frank kept picking at him. So Sam just kept trying to find a way to please his father. He played football, he worked construction, and he got good grades. I really thought when Sam got the football scholarship to University of Oklahoma, my uncle would finally tell him how proud he was. But, he didn't. He bragged on Sam to everyone else, but Uncle Frank never told Sam that he had done good. And I don't know if he ever told him he loved him once Sam was grown up." Naomi nodded at this too, as her fingers flew across her laptop's keyboard. She paused in her typing to look up when Bobbi sighed deeply, as if the next words she would say were too painful to speak.

"That summer after his junior year at Oklahoma, Sam was fooling around, riding wild ponies at the local rodeo, and he got thrown. Blew his knee out. There went football. Uncle Frank went crazy. Sam lost his scholarship, but he had enough saved from working summers and playing in his band to cover what he lost. Sam and his father didn't really speak for over a year. It wasn't until graduation that Sam tried to make it up with his dad, but my uncle never really forgave him. He died just before Sam signed his first record contract." Bobbi stopped and took a long sip from her water bottle. The eyes of the two women met in dawning realization of their shared histories.

Naomi muttered, "I had a father just like that. I was never good enough. But, given everything that happened to them, all they had been through in the Holocaust, my mother would never speak against him. She tried to smooth things over when she could, but she wouldn't—really, she couldn't—stand up to him for me. Just a month before my son was born, my father passed away. He never saw Jonah."

Neither woman spoke for several minutes. Naomi broke the silence by asking, "When did Sam get his first record deal?"

"Well, Sam had married up with Emily pretty much right out of college, but he was on the road constantly. He and Mickey and Beau and Tommy drove from town to town, bar to bar, taking any booking that was offered. Emily was working in Tulsa in a real estate office, and she tried to meet up with Sam when he was on the road for more than a few weeks. He said he wanted to give it two years. If he didn't have a record deal in two years, he'd quit and join his dad's construction company. But the two years became three, and he was still on the road. He was trying to play, to write, and to get home to Emily. But, he couldn't be everything to everyone, and he and Emily split up." Bobbi paused as if she wanted to add something. Instead, she just opened up the carpetbag at her feet and started pulling out yarn in a rainbow of colors.

"I was finished with college by then, and I joined up with him. We were playing one night at this old honky-tonk in Abilene when Tyrone Butler showed up. We were blown away! He played a bit with Sam and the boys and me. It was such a thrill. Tyrone had such a tremendous reputation even then that we couldn't believe he was taking an interest in us. The next day he pulled up in this old reconditioned school bus and asked Sam if he could tag along for a while. That was when things started happening. Tyrone knew just about everyone. He helped Sam and Mickey polish up some of their songs, and he found us some other material. We recorded some songs in this little studio in Houston, and then we just traveled around the Southwest and the South for the rest of the year. We brought that cassette with us, and it started to sell, and it started getting played on the radio. By the end of 1989, Sam had a contract with Nashville Records, just like that. Couldn't have done it without Tyrone. And Tommy. Why, when that boy got the chance, there was just no stopping him. He came up with promotional ideas, found us songs, booked us in every place he could find, and we started to get some attention."

JoEllen had been quiet through Bobbi's monologue, just nodding her head from time to time, but now she snorted at Bobbi's last statement, muttering, "Yeah. And as soon as you all had put in the hard work, Lola showed up. Perfect timing every time with that one."

Bobbi laughed, but it wasn't a pleasant sound either. "You got that one right, girlfriend. There are no flies on Lola, and there never was."

"Lola was Sam's second wife?" Naomi asked in an innocent tone. She knew exactly who Lola was and the part she had played in the band, but the undercurrents she felt rippling between Bobbi and JoEllen bespoke a much more interesting story than the one she had heard.

Rolling a ball of yarn from the skein she slipped over JoEllen's slender hands, in a way that made Naomi believe the two shared a deep friendship that was as strong and multihued as the yarn, Bobbi shook her head at Naomi.

"You all want to know any more about Lola, you'd best ask Tyrone, or wait until Lola shows up on the tour, and, believe me, she will. But don't ask Sam about Lola. He has a blind spot with that one." JoEllen just murmured her assent with that statement.

"Lola joined up because I took some time off to marry my Alan. He was back from the city—not New York, but Dallas—and was fed up with big business. He wanted to farm like his daddy so he brought himself and his business degree and all his experience home and became the farmer he was meant to be. He just had to get some wildness out of his system, that's all, or he never would have gone off after college."

JoEllen was laughing so hard at that last statement she pulled her hands out of the skein to hold her sides. "Alan!? Wild?! *Dear Jesus God*! Wild is never a word I'd use to describe Alan Bodine!" There were tears spilling out of her dark, almond shaped eyes, spotting the bright red T-shirt she wore.

"A lot you know, JoEllen," Bobbi huffed, as she picked up the fallen yarn. But she was smiling nonetheless, as if she had some secrets she was keeping to herself. Bobbi squealed with delight at the song playing on the radio.

"JoEllen, turn that up, girl." Bobbi urged her friend. "I love this song!" JoEllen complied and the joyous sound of the Dixie Chicks flowed through the bus. The two women joined in on the chorus of "Cowboy, Take Me Away."

"That Natalie sure can sing," remarked JoEllen as the song ended and she turned the radio down. Naomi smiled at their exuberance, and their unselfish praise of the other singer.

Bobbi nodded, adding, "I love that fiddle playing, too. Those girls are so talented. Damn, I wish Sam had written that song."

"Maybe we can get Sam to let us do it some night. Kind of *our favorites*. Maybe each of us could do a song by one of our favorite artists." JoEllen made notes, warming to the idea. "Bobbi, you could do the fiddle and sing, couldn't you?"

While the two women discussed this latest idea, Naomi focused again on her laptop, making more notes about her conversation with Bobbi. The dusty Texas landscape whizzed by beyond the darkened windows of the bus. It was like a traveling hotel suite, with a lounge in the front, equipped with an advanced music and video system, refrigerator, and microwave. Beyond that were bunks for the band members, two bathrooms and another sitting room at the back of the bus, with a computer and some sound equipment. Closing her laptop, Naomi turned back to Bobbi and asked how the current tour had come about.

Knitting an afghan as the flat miles stretched out ahead of them, Bobbi started by talking about Sam and his third wife, Beckie. Bobbi spoke softly of how Sam was always taking care of everyone else, but no one had taken care of Sam for some time.

"Well, Beckie, she sure catered to him, at least until Sarah was born. Then she didn't want to tour with him anymore. She just wanted to stay at his place outside of Tulsa and tend the baby. Of course, we were recording his *Double Live* album—ain't it strange how we still call them albums when nobody plays anything but CD's anymore? And he had to keep touring to get the recordings for the CD. That CD went platinum so many times, we just lost count."

"But, he was planning to slow down, when Beckie got pregnant again. Sarah was just three, and Sam decided he would stop touring for a while to be home with his little girl and the new baby. Sam was just thrilled there was going to be another child, and we had been touring for nearly two years straight, anyway. The album was almost complete, he was just looking for a few more recordings—he wasn't happy with a couple of the songs." Bobbi stopped and peered closely at Naomi. "You aren't gonna write that he was more interested in his career than in his family, are you? 'Cause that just wasn't how it was. He loved Beckie and that little girl. And he was planning on taking a year or two off after the baby was born. He'd already arranged for all of us, even the tour crew, to get paid while he was home."

"Of course not," Naomi reassured the other woman. "I didn't think of it like that, more like he was tying up loose ends so there would be no distractions while he was home with his family."

"You got it right, then." Bobbi's warm smile reached her dark blue eyes, so much like Sam's, but without his reserve.

She went back to her knitting, working the needles almost ferociously as she recounted for Naomi how Sam had left Beckie and Sarah at their home in Tulsa to go out on the road for just three more weeks, just seven shows. After that, he would be home for at least a year, doing the final editing of the live album at his home studio, and just being with his family. Then late one afternoon, Beckie drove into Tulsa for her monthly check-up and to do some shopping. She had Sarah in the car seat.

"Just like they say to." Bobbi's voice broke. "Some damn fool drunk ran a red light and plowed into them. Sarah was gone right off, but Beckie, she hung on for two days. Sam got back just before Beckie died. And their poor unborn baby was already gone from the impact of the car crash." Naomi was blinking back the tears burning her eyes. Bobbi's voice trailed off, she stopped knitting and looked out the window for so long Naomi wondered if she had lost her train of thought. JoEllen held Bobbi's hand, squeezing it from time to time, offering silent comfort. It was several minutes before Bobbi took up the sad tale again.

"Well, Sam, he just lost it. He ranted and raved for hours, and then he just got real quiet. He got his family buried, and then he left. He told Emily to sell the house and to get rid of everything in it. He didn't care what she did with it, just sell it and give the money to MADD, you know, Mothers Against Drunk Driving. Well, Emily—you'll probably meet her in Oklahoma City—she's a practical one. She took all of Sam's stuff, his awards, his sheet music, tapes, notes and such, and put them in one of those storage places. She packed some of Beckie's things for him and some of Sarah's, too. I don't know if he's ever even seen those things. They might still be in storage. I should ask Emily."

Bobbi sighed and shook her head at Naomi. Naomi was trying to blink away her own tears. "Most people only knew that Sam's wife and daughter had died in a car accident, the news that Beckie had been pregnant was kept out of the papers. It was as though everyone involved had known that information was just too private to release. I don't think you need to say anything about it either." Naomi had not heard this tragic piece of the story. It wrenched her heart

How had Sam survived this? But, he almost had not. Everyone knew he started drinking heavy then, out in Colorado, on the edge of nowhere. She nodded her head in agreement and Bobbi continued with the sad tale.

"Sam had this place in the Rockies, somewhere outside of Denver. He bought it from someone down on his luck that needed some quick money. It wasn't anything more than a hunting lodge or something like that. But Sam, he holed up there, with the housekeeper and her husband, and he started drinking. And building. He added on so many rooms that the place isn't even recognizable anymore. Did almost all the work himself—his daddy was a builder, remember? He can do a little bit of just about anything."

"Anyway, he drank and built for about a year. Tyrone and Mickey finished putting the live album together and the record company went ahead and released it. Sam said he didn't care what they did with it. Tyrone went out to see Sam a few times, but Sam wouldn't even let him in the door. Finally, Tyrone brought Tommy, and they just forced their way in. Sam had a beard, long hair—almost to his shoulders, can you believe it? They said he must have weighed about one hundred fifty pounds—just skin and bones—because Sam has always been a big boy, you know. Well, they just threw out all the tequila, sent the housekeeper away, and stayed with Sam until he sobered up.

"They were gone for almost six weeks, then Tommy came back. Tyrone stayed on with Sam. He was sick for a long time. And half out of his head. He had never done any grieving, really, for Beckie and Sarah and that poor unborn baby. He just drowned everything in tequila. So, he had to mourn them. He blamed himself, you see. I think he was trying to work or drink himself to death." Bobbi's voice was almost a whisper at the last.

"*Vas der mensch ken alts ibertrachten, ken der ergster soyna im nisht vinchen.*" Naomi murmured.

"What did you say? What does that mean?" Bobbi asked.

"It's Yiddish. My father used to say it about the survivors. It means, 'What people can think up for themselves, their own worst enemies wouldn't wish on them.' Many of the survivors blamed themselves, just like Sam, for having lived when so many others had died. And they punished themselves, worse than the Nazis had done."

"That's exactly right. No one blamed Sam, not even Beckie. But he couldn't see it." Bobbi shook her head in agreement. "Naomi, you might be a slick New York writer, but underneath, I think you are just folks." Naomi smiled shyly at the other woman, acknowledging the compliment.

"Sam kind of came back to himself that next year. He started writing a bit, and he and Tyrone and Tommy came up with the idea of this album and tour. People were coming by Sam's place to see how he was, and they would start fooling around with songs. Sam had built a small recording studio at the Colorado house, and they made some recordings. The record company liked it, the album sold a gazillion copies, and here we are. It was good for Sam to see that people still loved him and wanted to be with him. It kept his mind off the accident. Losing that baby, it was almost like that first time with Emily."

JoEllen broke in, "Bobbi, sometimes you just don't know when to be still. You don't have to go on about Emily to Naomi here. She doesn't need that for her article, do you, Naomi?"

"I certainly wouldn't mention it without Sam offering the information to me."

JoEllen Robideau had been less friendly to Naomi than Bobbi. The beautiful black woman was about her age, and she had been one of Sam's backup singers for several years. Naomi already noticed she spent a lot of time with Tommy. Bobbi told her JoEllen often drove Tommy's Navigator while he made endless calls on his cell phone. *There is a story there, too.* Naomi let her curiosity about that and her questions about Emily remain unspoken. She had to travel with the group for many more days. It would not do to alienate one of the few other women in the entourage this early in the game. Besides, Emily was supposed to be at the concert in Oklahoma City. *I'll corner her there… I'll get her to tell me what these two wouldn't.*

Sure enough, Emily Watson Rhodes Smith was in Oklahoma City—looking for all the world like a well-off, middle-aged, suburban matron. Which is what she was. She wandered backstage on the night of the concert with Walker, her thin, balding husband—who was also her real estate partner—in tow. Everyone in the band greeted her warmly. A short, slightly plump woman with beautiful hazel eyes, well-cut curly brown hair, and a wide smile, Emily had a way of touching each man and woman she met that said, "I like who I am and I like you, too."

When Sam came up to her it was different, though. They still love each other, Naomi thought, as Sam pulled Emily into his arms and just held her. Her arms wrapped around his waist, her hand patted his back. He bent to kiss her, and Naomi saw the tears in her eyes. Sam's big hands brushed the tears away. Then she laughed when he whispered something in her ear. Sam reached around her to shake Walker Smith's hand, and Naomi saw the respect each man had for the other. *What kind of man is this who has an ex-wife who still loves him after almost twenty years and the second husband who treats him like a younger brother?*

Sam introduced Naomi to Emily and Walker. Emily gave Naomi a speculative look as Sam described her as a "slick writer from New York City." Naomi smiled derisively at that remark.

"Well, now, Sam, I'm really just a small town girl myself. I grew up in upstate New York. I've only lived in the City for nine years." Naomi shook hands with Emily as she spoke. Emily's face softened. Naomi knew she didn't look *small-town* in black leather and denim, but she didn't sound *New York* either. Naomi followed Emily's gaze and met Sam's steely blue eyes, trained on her. Sam quickly turned his attention to Walker, and they wandered off to review some papers the older man pulled out of a beaten up leather portfolio. Emily turned to Naomi. "Why don't we go sit over by the food, Naomi, and you can tell me what Sam doesn't like about you being here."

"Well, he certainly seems to have an aversion to *city girls*, especially *New York*, as he so charmingly refers to me. And he doesn't like to answer questions, either. But, I can get around that." Naomi sighed. She really didn't know why Sam seemed to dislike her or why he was able to get her back up quicker than anyone she knew, with the possible exception of the blood-sucking lawyer.

"He's short with you because he's attracted to you and he doesn't want to be." Emily replied as though she was explaining something to a very slow eight-year-old.

Naomi snorted, unladylike, but effective. "Attracted to me? He's about as attracted to me as he is to…to…poison ivy!" she exclaimed.

"Well, you certainly have given him an itch." Emily chuckled. "Look, Sam doesn't want to complicate his life with relationships.

Every time he's had feelings for a woman, its spelled disaster for him. He shies away from new people now, not that he was ever the most outgoing person. Why, when I first knew him at college, he was so shy, I had to ask him for a date." Emily reached for a pitcher of iced tea and poured a glass for herself and one for Naomi.

"How much do you know about Sam anyway, Naomi?"

"Well, I know he sang in church as a kid and he started playing guitar in college—that must have been when you two were together. And then he started traveling around with a small band, playing anywhere that would have him."

"He played for beer and peanuts, basically. They drove around in an old pick-up truck of Tommy's and Sam's red Mustang. I think Sam still has that car out at the Colorado house." Emily was smiling softly, as she started her trip down memory lane. This was what Naomi was so good at—getting people to open up and then just letting them tell their stories. She listened attentively to what was said, and more important, what was left unsaid.

"He was always something, Sam was. He was so handsome then, not so harsh looking as he is now. I always thought he had the most beautiful blue eyes, like blue fire. And he was such a gentleman. Some girls would have taken advantage of him then, but I didn't. I loved him almost from the start." There was a wistful smile playing around Emily's lips.

"I'm a practical one. I didn't think the band would make it. Not that they didn't have talent, but there are so many bands, so many songwriters, that most never get a record deal—most barely make a living. I figured Sam would give it up after a couple of years and we could settle down. I was willing to wait but Sam, but he wanted to get married right after school, and well, I never could say no to Sam. I went to work in Walker's real estate office, and I met Sam on weekends whenever I could. It was an adventure for those boys. Sam and Mickey and Tommy really loved playing at honkytonks and county fairs. You know, Sam still plays some county fairs on every tour, just to stay in touch with the folks." Naomi sat and listened as Sam's first love spun their tale.

"That's the way things went for about three years, a year longer than Sam said he would keep trying to get a record deal. I wasn't happy, I was alone most of the time. I had an English degree and thought I might teach, but we needed money to live on, and there weren't many teaching jobs in those days. So I took the job with Walker, studied for my license, and found I had a knack for selling houses. But, you know, most houses are shown on the weekend, so I couldn't take off to be with Sam. The time between visits just got longer and longer. Sam was out there chasing his dream, and I just couldn't follow him."

She was silent for a long moment, as if she was considering just how much to tell Naomi. The sadness that stole across Emily's face was visible. Naomi could almost hear Emily's mind working through whatever dilemma she was trying to resolve. Discretion must have won out because Emily concluded her narrative by saying she and Sam drifted apart and had really been too young to marry in the first place. Their divorce had been amicable, and then Walker declared his long-hidden love for Emily. They had been married for over ten years.

The two women sat quietly for a few minutes, sipping sweet tea. Naomi's eyes followed Sam as he moved through the backstage area: talking to the band, picking on Tommy by pulling his headset off and tossing it to Tyrone in a highly technical game of keep-away. Then he was stopping to give autographs and have pictures taken with the fans who made it backstage one way or the other, and drinking the gallons of bottled water he consumed every night before he took the stage. Emily broke the silence.

"What are you really doing here, Naomi?" Subtlety was lost on Emily.

"My editor thought it would be a good idea for me to tour with the band so I could write a first-hand account on the country star phenomenon who was being played on every damn station in the country, and who was nightly filling arenas and convention centers with fans from every walk of life, age group, and income level." She delivered her pat response to Emily's question without even taking a breath.

Emily raised her eyebrow at Naomi's recitation.

Naomi laughed out loud. Out of the corner of her eye, she saw Sam's head turn toward her. His eyes—those blue eyes, blue like the ice on her beloved Adirondacks in the middle of winter when it was so cold the water tumbling from the rocks became frozen sapphire—narrowed to frigid slits. *Was it the man or was it his past that had turned him to ice?*

She turned away from Sam and caught a knowing smile just before it disappeared from Emily's face. Then Sam's first wife winked at her. *Damn if she didn't really like Emily.*

"He's magic, isn't he?" Naomi leaned toward Emily. "He has a really beautiful voice and quite a range. But that isn't it; there are singers with better voices. There is something about him. I've only seen it a few times, but he holds an audience in the palm of his hand, doesn't he? And he cares about that. Last night, I saw him watching their faces as they were watching him. It's like he's looking for something from them…approval, I think."

Naomi rested her elbows on her knees and clasped her hands, staring down at her fists as she tried to find the words she was looking for. She had not been able to properly express these thoughts on her laptop, either. Frowning in concentration, she finally said, "No, it's something simpler…acceptance. And when he gets it, his face is transformed and his voice just soars…" Naomi's voice trailed off when she looked up from her hands and saw the unshed tears in Emily's eyes.

"How did you figure that out in just two days? It took some of us years to learn that much about Sam." Emily patted Naomi's fisted hands.

"But that's not all of it, is it? I'm missing something. I feel like he's always just out of my reach." Naomi ran her hands through the tangled mass of her hair, lifting it away from her face and then up from her neck, in concentration, in frustration. She stopped with her hands buried in her hair when she noticed Sam staring at her. Again. His quizzical look quickly replaced by something else— frustration, tension, annoyance—before the mask slipped back into place; the good, ole, friendly Sam mask. His hands reached for his curly black hair, spiking it up, slicking it down—it would always spring back up in the unruly curls that were his trademark, along with the faded jeans, baby grand piano, and beat-up guitar.

Emily's voice tore Naomi's gaze away from Sam but did nothing to quiet the flutters in her gut. "You just stick with it, honey. You're on the right track. But have a care with him, he bruises easy, and he won't let you know that. There's some that he's got to tell you himself, if you really want to know about Sam Rhodes. I hope you find what you're looking for, and I don't mean just a cover story."

Emily stood and walked away before Naomi could protest all she was looking for *was* the story.

Throughout the show, Naomi stayed off to the right, Sam's side of the stage, her eyes never leaving him. This was a home crowd for the Oklahoma boy, and he was savoring it. And they truly loved the mystery guest—Bonnie Raitt—when she stepped up to the mic with Sam. He introduced her as his favorite redhead, and he drew a laugh from the crowd when he asked, "None of you have seen Lola lurking around here, have you? She still thinks *she's* my favorite redhead! No? You're right, only one ex-wife here tonight—my favorite ex-wife—Emily Rhodes Smith." The spotlight found Emily and she smiled and waved to the crowd. It appeared to be a familiar routine for Sam and Emily. The fans whooped and cheered.

Sam had a habit of talking a bit before almost every song. He said, with his arm around Bonnie, "Have you ever loved someone who didn't love you back? Nothing you said or did could change it, could it? And one day, you just had to give up the fight, knowing you would love the person until you died, knowing the other person cared, but not enough. And so, you let the person go. Bonnie sure got it right with this song."

He moved away from her to play the beautiful piano intro for "I Can't Make You Love Me", as Bonnie started singing. The hair on Naomi's neck stood up as the light played across Sam's face, across his hands dancing over the keyboard. Heartbreak was written on his granite features, and his voice—when he joined Bonnie on the chorus—was filled with sadness and longing. She and everyone else in the audience had tears in their eyes when the song finished with those few plaintive notes.

The rest of the set rocked. Sam and Bonnie were having as much fun as the audience with "Let's Give Them Something to Talk About", acting out the suggestive lyrics and laughing in each other's arms at the end. Sam was an accomplished singer and guitarist and played the piano beautifully, but that was not all. He was the consummate showman, giving his fans everything they hoped for and then a little bit more.

Standing alone in the wings, Naomi was deep in thought. *He puts so much emotion into every song, how does he have anything left at the end of the show? Is that why he seems so remote at times?* Naomi still did not have any answers, even after the third encore.

CHAPTER FOUR

On the road again... Naomi shrugged her stiff shoulders as she climbed aboard Sam's bus in the early morning hours. It had been ten days since she had flown into Dallas, and her *tush* was feeling every mile of it. *I'm getting too old for this shit*, she thought disgustedly. The tour had taken them to Memphis from Oklahoma City, then on to Louisville, and Indianapolis. In each city, the reception Sam and his band received had been the same: sell-out crowds at every arena or amphitheater, rock and country stars dropping by as if they were stopping off at an old friend's house for an evening of small talk. Melissa Etheridge had been with Sam in Memphis, and they tore the roof off the concert hall with their version of Springsteen's "Thunder Road."

Naomi rolled her neck and shrugged her shoulders again, trying to get some relief before she just dumped her black leather bag and laptop on the nearest of the swivel recliners grouped together in the front third of the bus. She had only been on Sam's bus once before in the days she traveled with the band. Sam had been tense and mostly uncommunicative. *I hope I have better luck today. It will be a hell of an article with no quotes from the damn subject of the piece.*

Sam emerged from the early morning mist and made his way past Charlie, the driver. Looking tired, but so appealing in his standard outfit of faded denims and a white T-shirt, a ratty baseball cap pulled down low, and black Ray-bans hanging from the cord around his neck, his eyes were weary but beautiful within the thick black fringe of his long lashes. He moved slowly but with innate grace, his big frame loose and athletic. Naomi could feel the now familiar tightening low in her belly, the hardening of her nipples, and the faint blush creeping up her neck. *How does he manage to rev me up just by appearing?* Naomi shifted uneasily in her seat. She had never had such an immediate physical reaction to any man, and it made her damned uncomfortable. *God, it's been so long since I was with anyone I don't know how to feel.*

Sam dropped his duffel bag at her feet and slumped into the black leather recliner adjacent to hers. He viewed her warily from under the brim of his cap, his eyes cold and appraising.

She wore her *work clothes*: black jeans, white T-shirt, black leather jacket, and beat-up red cowboy boots. Sam felt himself harden at the sight of those long, black-clad legs stretched out into the aisle. She certainly wasn't pretty, she had an attitude just this side of bitchy, and he didn't trust for a minute the words she was punching into that laptop or the feelings that were flooding his system. So, he opted for rude and slightly sneering.

"What is it with you and the cowboy boots, *New York*? A subtle put-down of the *good ole boys* you're being forced to spend time with?" Even to himself he sounded as grumpy as he felt. *What is it about the woman that sets my teeth to grinding and my pulse pounding?*

"Nope, *Cowboy*, just a little personal statement I decided to make a few years ago. A warning that I am capable of kicking ass and taking names if I have to." Naomi retorted.

The bus started pulling away from the hotel as the two sat in silence, staring out opposite windows. For the first time, they were almost alone on the bus, Bobbi and the guys sleeping on the other bus and JoEllen driving Tommy's Navigator, with William in the backseat. Only Tyrone was in the back of Sam's bus, listening to music on his headset while he thumbed through the newest issue of *American Cowboy*.

Naomi broke the silence. "So, Sam, you gonna talk to me today?" she asked softly. Her wistful voice made him look away from the skyline already shimmering in the heat of the July morning, sliding away as the bus sped toward Chicago. He was so tired, and there were still eight or nine more cities and hundreds of miles before the next break in the tour. Once again he questioned the wisdom of taking the band back on the road. *I'm getting too old for this shit.*

Gritting his teeth, he forced himself to answer the quiet question with as much civility as possible, His momma had raised him to be polite to women, all women, even a nosy, clever, and too-sexy-for-her-own-good woman from New York City.

"What do you want to know? Seems like you've talked to everybody about this show and album. You and Bobbi always have your heads together; you probably know more about me than I know about myself."

"Bobbi only tells me the good stuff about you, Sam. She's such a *zise nishumele*; she'd never say anything bad about you. And I bet there's plenty of bad to tell."

"What does that mean, what you just said?" he asked, leaning toward her.

"What? Oh, that. It's Yiddish and means 'gentle soul'. Someone who wouldn't hurt a fly."

"That would be Bobbi, she's been defending me her whole life."

"Defending you from whom?"

"Mostly from myself, I guess. After all, aren't we our own harshest critics, *New York*?" Sam asked, peering up from under his cap.

"Okay, *Cowboy* so, we're going to be philosophical today?" Naomi sighed. Another round of verbal jousting with Sam was surely going to push her over the edge.

"Yes, ma'am." He was grinning at her now, that *Sam* grin, self-deprecating and slightly mischievous.

"Well, Sam, what makes you so special? Why are you getting so much attention after twenty years of recording and touring?"

"Hell, New York, I've been getting attention for nearly twenty years from my fans, it's just recently that you *city folk* have taken notice of me. Must be 'cause I'm hanging around with the big boys, like Springsteen," Sam answered sarcastically.

"You have to admit you're bringing out some big stars to sing with you, stars who have their own fans who have not necessarily been *your* fans, if they had even heard of you," she persisted.

"Did you ever think that maybe I'm introducing *my* fans to the music of other singers, not that other singers are bringing their fans to me? No. Because I'm *country*, so naturally no one who listens to rock or blues or alternative music would be interested in my songs. You people are so damn pretentious!" He pulled off his baseball cap and began raking his fingers through his hair in his now-familiar gesture of frustration or anger—or both. His face was hard, and his eyes were fading into that ice blue that froze her out at their first meeting. But, at least she had gotten a reaction from him.

"You put on a helluva show, *Cowboy.* I'll admit that; but you have to admit, from a public relations standpoint, this tour is an innovative moneymaker."

"Yes, it is. But you think of this tour in terms of money and exposure. I think of it in terms of respect and gratitude and sharing myself with my fans. I'm coming out of a bad time in my life." Sam paused and looked out the window, composing himself. The muscle along his jawline was working, as he clenched then relaxed his teeth. He turned back to her. "When I was down and almost out, the fans were still there. I got cards, letters, telegrams, e-mails, everything. With prayers and wishes for my health and happiness. Some people even sent me money—I guess they thought I needed it because I wasn't working." He shook his head as if he still could not believe it, and the gesture went straight to Naomi's heart.

"People in the industry called and visited, too. I didn't know about a lot of it initially because I was drinking pretty heavy for a while there after Beckie...after...the accident...." His voice trailed off as pain streaked across his face. Those brilliant blue eyes faded to an almost colorless gray. "You know, Eric Clapton sent me a letter about losing his son. That meant so much...he said I had to keep on and I couldn't drown the pain because it would always be there; I had to face it. And I had to make Sarah proud of me." He paused. "Don't write about that, okay?" Naomi nodded her assent to his request, unable to speak after hearing the echoes of raw emotion in his voice.

"Anyway, after a time, people started coming by, and we would noodle around with my songs and their songs and other songs we liked as a way of relaxing and, I guess, of getting me back to the music. I started writing then, I hadn't written much in the last three years...." The restless hands were clenching and unclenching on his lap. He sighed deeply, and then the sad smile disappeared from his lips, replaced by an irreverent grin.

"So, now I'm back on the road, making music with singers I like and respect and giving the fans songs they might not have heard before, and I'm sharing a little of myself with them like they shared with me. You can tell a lot about a person by the music they like and listen to. Like you. What's one of your favorite songs?" Sam threw the question out as a challenge, not an inquiry.

"'I Will Survive'," Naomi blurted out before she realized how much of herself she had revealed in that one answer. Sam's eyebrow went up, then his eyes narrowed as if he was seriously considering her answer. *Oh yeah, that tells a lot about the cool Ms. Stein, a whole lot.*

"I mean, "Thunder Road" and "Running On Faith" and anything by the Beatles and Tina......." Her cheeks were burning and the words just tumbled out. *Damn the man,* he could get her flustered faster than any man she had ever met; even the blood-sucking lawyer.

"I like those songs, too. See how much we have in common? That's what I mean about this tour, it's sharing a part of me with my fans who have been letting me into their lives for years, and maybe it's introducing me to some people who didn't know me before. What is wrong with that? If you are a musician, you are always looking for an audience. It doesn't work if you are only singing your songs to yourself. You have to put yourself out there and see if you touch anyone," Sam concluded, with a shrug of his broad shoulders.

She knew what he meant. Everything she wrote was a test she forced herself to take. She knew she wrote well, but she, too, wanted to reach people, to make them see what she saw, feel what she felt. And sometimes, she got the response she was looking for: she made somebody feel something they hadn't felt before, think about something or someone in a way they had never considered before. Acceptance and approval. If only she could receive that from people she loved. Maybe that was what Sam was looking for too.

Naomi glanced over at the silent man sitting across from her. He had pulled his sunglasses on and was gazing out the window as the ever-changing American landscape rolled by: city streets giving way to arterials, then to highways, speeding through suburbs and country, rivers and valleys, never-changing and ever-changing. *How many thousands of miles have I ridden and never really seen the country?* Usually her eyes focused on the blinking green cursor on her laptop or on the bored eyes of some singer or musician. She sighed.

"I can't carry a tune, but I still used to sing "Sweet Baby James" to my son when he was little."

Sam pushed the sunglasses down his nose and stared at her. She saw his eyes widen and warm to a deep cerulean blue. He didn't look away and she couldn't. It was as though they were seeing each other for the first time.

"I sang that to my little girl, too."

With those words, a truce was reached between them. A tentative truce, but one that made the silence enveloping them comfortable for the first time since Texas.

Naomi thought the trip to Chicago would be uneventful. But the bus pulled off the Interstate just across the Illinois line. She looked around and was just about to ask the reason they were making an unscheduled stop when Tyrone came rushing up from the back of the bus. As he brushed by her, Tyrone said "Little lady, you are about to enjoy the best sweet potato pie outside the South."

Sam was already off the bus and hustling through the door of a small roadside café with a faded sign proclaiming "Rosie's Café—Best Pies Anywhere". Naomi gathered her bag and followed the crew inside. She saw Sam go right into the kitchen and lift a tiny, thin black woman at the stove into his arms for a whopping hug and kiss. Tyrone was right behind him. *This has to be Rosie.* The woman shooed the two men who dwarfed her out of the kitchen and sat them at a large round table by the window. Within minutes, steaming cups of coffee and thick slices of pie arrived, brought to them by a sweet-faced young woman, who wore the old woman's smile.

Rosie introduced her younger counterpart as her grandbaby, Cynthia, who was helping out while she was home for the summer from Tulane University. Cynthia hugged Sam and Tyrone, before she and JoEllen put their heads together about some truly amazing shopping spree they were planning for the next time JoEllen was in New Orleans. Rosie came to sit with them, still directing other customers to empty tables and ordering the wait staff to top off their cups and bring the boys more pie.

In between bites of creamy pie, Naomi asked Rosie how Sam had become acquainted with her.

"Well, it was quite a few years ago. He wasn't a whole lot older than Cynthia is now. He and some of his boys were driving around playing in any place that would have them. They were trying their luck here in Indiana when Tommy's truck broke down. My late husband, Mr. DeParois, was alive then, and we had us a little garage and coffee shop not far from here. He fixed up that truck for Sam and Tommy and Mickey and we let them bunk down on our sleeping porch. They didn't have enough money between them to pay for the repairs, but my husband said as how they were good Christian boys, we ought to trust them. It wasn't a week later that an envelope arrived with what they owed him. After that, whenever they were in the area, they stopped by. Started bringing Tyrone with them the next year in that old school bus." Rosie turned toward Sam as she asked, "Whatever happened to that bus, Sam?"

"Tyrone has it parked on his farm. He decked it out as a den or something when he needs to get away from all those females at his house. Tyrone has three girls and the sweetest wife in Texas, don't you, Hoss?" Tyrone merely shrugged as he inhaled a second piece of Rosie's pie. Rosie's faded eyes twinkled as she patted his arm, obviously appreciating his appetite, before she continued her story.

"Well, a few years later, this place came up for sale. We really wanted to buy it 'cause it is just off the Interstate, and we thought we could turn it into a real truckers' stop. Make us some good money. Sam loaned us the money when the banks wouldn't even talk to us. Two old black folks, didn't even have a high school education between us, nobody thought we could do it, except Sam."

Sam looked away at Rosie's words, a slow blush creeping up his neck. "No need to go on about it now, darlin'. It was a good investment, and you paid back every cent."

"Which you turned around and gave Cynthia for college." Rosie retorted.

"Well, it was just a little high school graduation present. She already had most of her money from scholarships," Sam said, somewhat abashed at the old woman's words.

"You're a good boy, Samuel, you just don't want anyone to

know it, acting like some *bad-ass* all the time, when I know your momma raised you right. You have a good heart, and nobody can tell me any different, not even you. You know I love you."

"I love you too, darlin', you're the only one for me." The endearment flowed easily from Sam's mouth, but his eyes flattened as he said the words. Rosie smiled gently and just patted his hand.

Naomi mulled over the conversation during the final few hours on the bus. She wanted to use the story in her article, but she was having a difficult time putting the words down. Sam was gruff and sometimes sarcastic, but he was also obviously generous and warm-hearted. A successful recording artist and songwriter, he seemed genuinely surprised by the outpouring of love from his fans and the respect of his fellow artists. *The man is a contradiction, but then, what interesting man isn't?* Naomi couldn't help but feel there was something else just out of her reach. *I must just be tired. It's good we'll be in Chicago late in the afternoon, I can sit down and write and catch up on my e-mail.*

Naomi got no writing done once she checked into the hotel because several angry messages from Jonah needed replies. *More trouble. Only a couple more weeks until he gets out of camp and can go to his father's. I hope, I hope David doesn't fuck this up.* Her shoulders sagged at the thought of everything that could go wrong with Jonah while she was on the road. She was so tired of dealing with men's shit. Her son, his father, and a difficult but tempting man from Oklahoma. She gave up on the notion of working on her article.

Oh, well. Maybe I can get some lingerie washed tonight. I wonder if Bobbi has any Woolite.

CHAPTER FIVE

Sam slammed the door behind him, following Naomi across her suite and into the bathroom. She was standing by the sink with her hands already in soapy water. He looked in the mirror and saw the bright splashes of red across her cheeks. *What the hell does she have to be angry about?* In two steps he was behind her, grabbing her by the shoulders. She looked up into the mirror, appearing startled by the blue fire she could see burning in his eyes.

"What the hell do you think you're doing with my boys?" he snarled at her. Sam was furious. His jaw clenched so tight he could feel his teeth grinding as he tried to control his temper. But even as his anger flared, part of his mind questioned: was he angry at Naomi or at himself?

"I was borrowing some Woolite from the *boys* to wash my underwear," Naomi retorted. Now, *she* was furious. "How dare you come into JoEllen's room and start spitting at me about drinking tequila with three men and two women, all of whom are over twenty-one!"

"You know you weren't just drinking tequila. You were coming on to Beau when I walked in. Letting him put his mouth on you like some tart!" It was an image burned into Sam's mind: Naomi, giggling, her shirt off one shoulder, while Beau bent over her, both of them with shot glasses in their hands. Mickey and Chase passing a bottle of tequila to Bobbi while JoEllen was handing slices of lime to the laughing twosome.

"Tart? What century are you living in, Sam? I was showing him how we did body shots in college; he had never done them. He was licking some salt off my shoulder, for God's sake! You're acting like he had his hand in my bra! "

"Bra! You aren't even wearing one!" He almost spat the words.

Naomi looked at him with fire in her eyes and, soapy hands notwithstanding, lifted up the hem of her sweatshirt to show him the strapless white bra she wore beneath. His jaw dropped as she pulled the sweatshirt back in place, but not before he saw her full breasts almost spilling out of the white lace. The neckline of her shirt still hung off one shoulder. He gasped in surprise when she said, "I haven't walked out of my room without a bra on since I was sixteen! I was never built for the bra-less look."

His hands tightened on her shoulders as they stared each other down in the mirror.

"Well, hell, that's not what it looked like to me. I walked in and there you were, a shot glass in your hand and his mouth on you, and you were looking like you were enjoying every minute of it!" He was pissed at her and even more pissed at himself for the way he was acting, but he couldn't get his temper under control. And he was hard, had gotten hard the minute she flashed her bra at him. And that just pissed him off more.

And even before she spoke, Sam knew Naomi was getting good and pissed too.

"How dare you tell me how to act? I am fucking sick and tired of men telling me what I can and cannot do. God! From my father to my ex-husband, now even my twelve-year old son, if they have a penis they think they can order me around. I am done taking men's shit." Sam took a step back and started to speak, but Naomi cut him off.

"I *was* enjoying it! He's a good kid. He's sweet and funny and misses his girl back home something fierce. We were talking about some love poems he could e-mail to her. Does it sound to you like I'm trying to seduce him? I'm probably old enough to be his mother!"

"You don't look like *anybody's* mother in that sweatshirt and those cut-offs." Sam growled. "You look like a teenage boy's wet dream."

Naomi blushed at the raw compliment. She started to answer Sam, but Sam silenced her when his mouth came down on her shoulder.

She tastes like Tequila and lime, and the memory of a thousand shots snaked through him, like a river of fire. She was salt and sweet and once he tasted her, he couldn't get enough. His hot kiss became a wet, sucking bite, devouring her.

Naomi stood silent and still. Sam felt a tremor pass through her. Then her head dropped to one side, giving him access to the smooth skin of her long neck. Her quickly indrawn breath was all the encouragement Sam needed. It had been three years since he had wanted a woman. And he wanted Naomi. His lips trailed from her neck to her jawline, branding her with hot wet kisses, his teeth scraping her skin.

Sam watched her in the mirror, watching both of them, through eyes narrowed to slits by desire. When Naomi's tongue flicked across her lips, he stifled a groan of his own. His hands left her shoulders, one reaching to turn her face toward him as he captured her mouth in a bruising kiss.

Naomi's lips parted slightly, as a sigh escaped, his tongue touched her lower lip; sliding past her teeth, breaching her defenses. She moaned, trying to twist toward him, but Sam held her fast, her bottom pressed against his hardening erection. His other hand had moved from her shoulder, down to her waist, then up under her sweatshirt.

Naomi sucked in her breath when he spread his hand across her belly. She was soft and warm. And he hardened at the thought of sinking into her woman's body. Her whole body tensed. She started to pull away from him, but he whispered against her lips, "Don't, don't. Please let me. Let me hold you, let me touch you…" before he returned to her mouth.

Pushing both of them to the limit, Sam swept his hands across her lush curves. When he brushed a hand over her breast, Naomi arched into his palm, as if seeking the sweet feel of his hand on her. His fingers plucked at her nipple, already hard and straining for his touch.

Sam was thinking, just barely, that he had to stop, that it was crazy to go down this road. She was a journalist doing a story, for Chrissake, not some over-eager groupie, and his days of tumbling groupies were long past. But, God, she felt so good, and those sexy little whimpers told him she liked what he was doing. The way she ground that beautiful ass into him told him she was as hot as he was.

"Naomi…darlin'…if you want me to stop, tell me, *now*," he

murmured into her ear, teasing that perfect shell. He felt her shiver then she melted further into his arms.

"Don't," she gasped.

No! Anguish washed over him at the idea of letting her go. His hands were full of her: one cupping her breast and the other fisted into that glorious mane of hair. Sam's caresses slowed, though. He had asked her and if she didn't want this insanity to go any further, he would respect her wishes. He hated himself for being stupid enough to ask, but he would stop.

"Don't...stop. Please, don't stop now." Naomi moaned as she reached for him.

It was awkward; he had her pinned to him, back to front, and his grip was like steel. She managed to reach an arm up and around his neck, pulling his head down to hers. His lips slid over her mouth and she sank her teeth into his bottom lip. *He* was groaning now. Her tongue swept past his teeth to mate with his tongue. Sam's whole body jerked involuntarily into her. He could feel her reaching for him and he hardened to bursting as her hand found him. She measured him, stroking up and down, against his fly.

That did it for him. Sam had reached—and passed—his limit. He pulled his mouth away from Naomi's and reached around her to unsnap her cut-offs and pull her zipper down. The too-big shorts fell to the floor, revealing a white lace thong. "Jesus, don't you have any regular underwear?" he swore.

Sam met Naomi's glazed eyes in the mirror. The woman he saw reflected in the bright glare looked like fast, hot, sex incarnate. Sam pulled at his belt buckle, his fingers stumbling.

"Let me," Naomi said, trying to turn to him.

"Don't move," he growled.

Finally, he was free of his jeans. Sam's erection pressed against her sweet bottom. He didn't know how long he could control himself. He looked at her in the mirror and knew he wasn't going to be able to hold on for much longer. Naomi's hair tousled around her face and shoulders; her mouth was wet and red, her lips swollen from their bruising kisses. Her sweatshirt was in disarray, the neck hanging off one shoulder, the bottom edge bunched above her breast, exposing all that heaving, creamy flesh and white lace. He looked at the soft curve of her belly and the curls of dark blonde hair below exposed by the skimpy panty she wore.

She was watching him watching her. Her eyes drooped closed as she moaned and, arching her back, rubbed her ass against him again.

Sam shook; his hand trembled as he reached into her panties, sliding the thin piece of elastic aside as his fingers found her. *God, she is so wet.* His finger slid inside, feeling the sleek, hot honey seeping from her. She moaned again as his thumb flicked the hot core of her. She thrust herself against him, starting to convulse around his finger. *She's so tight.*

His erection throbbed. *Now,* Sam growled. He guided himself between her legs. She bent forward, resting her arms on the vanity. His hand still cupped her sex, rubbing her tiny hardness, while the head of his erection pushed against her. She arched her back a little and he felt himself slide into her, slowly, a fraction of an inch at a time. She moved her legs apart a little more to give him room and he rewarded her with the long, hard feel of him as he went in deep, buried to the hilt.

Sam breathed hard now, gasping, as though he had run the mile at record speed. *Nothing has ever felt this good, nothing.* She was hotter and wetter than any woman he'd ever had. He withdrew a bit and her inner muscles clutched the length of him, as if begging him to stay inside her. Moving into her again, Sam held on, one hand twined in the curls at the apex of her legs, holding her and rubbing her. His other hand grasped her hip in a bruising grip, holding on for his life.

"Come for me, baby." Sam whispered. "I want to see you come. I want you to see it. Open your eyes, Naomi, and look at us."

Naomi raised her head and opened those cat eyes. What she saw seemed to push her over the edge. Sam strained behind her, every cord on his neck standing out, the muscles on his arms bunched. His tanned skin was in stark relief to her much paler body especially his hand disappearing into the snow white of her panties. Then he thrust into her again, all the way in, and his name exploded from her bruised lips.

What is happening to me? It never felt like this, never felt this good. Naomi was on fire, her muscles clutched him, her hips jerking in a staccato rhythm. And as she came, her liquid fire rained down on him, her inner grip as tight around him as his grip on her hips.

He raced to meet her, holding her hard against him as his own climax began. He gushed into her, like lava erupting from an exploding volcano. He filled her with flesh and fire for what seemed like forever. He thought he cried out her name. Then they were still.

Sam collapsed against Naomi, sucking in great gulps of air, shuddering with the violence of their orgasms. Little aftershocks ran through her, caressing him, as he slowly withdrew. The air in the bathroom was steamy with sweat and sex.

Naomi lifted her head, a smug, satisfied smile started to play across her lips, until she focused on Sam's face. He felt shell-shocked, as if he didn't know quite who or where he was. Her smile faded as he spoke.

"Oh, God, Naomi, I'm sorry."

He was already pulling on his jeans. He couldn't look at her face. All he could see were the bruises already blooming on her hip. He had hurt her. He had never, physically, hurt a woman. Sam fumbled with her panties, trying to right them, while he reached for her shorts, pulling them up her long legs. He faltered when he saw the creamy liquid on her inner thighs, further evidence of his transgression. *Jesus! I'm an animal!* He hadn't even thought of protection, for her or for him. He had taken her standing up, like a stallion mounting a mare at his ranch. No thought for anyone but himself. And he'd left marks on her!

Naomi stared at him. Sam finally looked at her, taking in the consternation on her face. *Oh, God, she hates me. She probably thinks I run around fucking every woman I meet. She doesn't know that there hasn't been anyone in three years. And when she sees those bruises, she'll think I'm some kind of Neanderthal who can't control himself. I have so totally fucked this up.*

"Sam...Sam, it's all right. I won't write anything about this. I won't...."

He cut her off. *Does she think I'm worried about myself?* "Naomi, I'm just sorry. I'm so sorry." He touched the bruise on her hip, shook his head, and walked out of the bathroom, his head hung low.

Bewildered, Naomi looked back in the mirror. What was it the guys in high school used to say? *She's been rode hard and put to bed wet.* Well, that's what she looked like, disheveled and in disarray. Her jean shorts hung open on her hips, her sweatshirt was still bunched above one breast, her lips swollen and red. She did believe, *yes*, there was a love bite on her shoulder.

There had been one boy her first year in college. A nice Jewish boy she met at a Hillel meeting. They studied together for weeks before he made a move, an inept, eager move too many glasses of wine had caused her to accept, more out of curiosity and affection than any lustful urges. He was awkward and inexperienced, and she never could figure out what all the sex fuss was about. It was messy and left her a little sore and more than a little embarrassed by the speed of his climaxes and his total lack of understanding that she had not "come as hard as he had."

Then David had entered her life. Sexy and self-assured, she had at first been suspicious of what he wanted from her. Naomi had long been sensitive about her abundant breasts and curved tush. But he pursued her for weeks, until she finally came to believe his statements of love and desire. By the spring, she would have done anything for him. He was a better lover than the first boy, but still, more often than not, he was finished before she had even begun. It never occurred to her to question his technique, assuming her lack of orgasms was her fault, not his. It took years before she had the nerve to ask him to take a little more time with her. His response, that she was obviously cold because no other woman had ever complained about his lovemaking, shut her up as he had intended. On rare occasions, when they had been drinking, he took it slow enough to satisfy her, so she had finally felt an orgasm. Then pregnancy and childbirth, nursing an infant and the changes in her body, had changed her wants and desires. And David had lost interest in her body. She was no longer attractive enough to really turn him on, which he had told her often enough.

Well, she had definitely done it for Sam, in ratty cut-offs and an old Cornell sweatshirt. She looked at herself in the mirror. She was soft, she didn't have the washboard abs of a gym enthusiast. Her less than perfect figure criticized too often by her ex-husband should have made her unable to relax in the harsh light of the bathroom and the unforgiving clarity of the mirror. But, Sam was heat, he was hard, and *he* had wanted *her*. That incredibly sexy, masculine creature had wanted her!

The thought made her smile, a slow, satisfied smile she watched creep across her face in the mirror. It had been a long time, a very long time, since she had made love. There had only been one brief encounter after her divorce, and it left her confused and even more unsure of herself as a woman. But, just now with Sam, she was certain he had been as overwhelmed by their lovemaking as she was. She giggled. *That was not making love, honey, that was good, old-fashioned fucking.* Well, she couldn't remember when she had ever been taken care of so thoroughly. Certainly never by the blood-sucking lawyer. His idea of thoroughly satisfying sex had been getting a blowjob!

Naomi started humming as she rinsed out the last few pieces of lingerie in the sink and hung them on the shower rod to dry. She was damned if Sam's guilt was going to make her feel bad or second-guess what had happened. Sex had never been like this before, and she was going to savor every bit of it, from the tangles in her hair down to the soreness she was already feeling between her legs. She knew there were women who bragged about earth-shattering climaxes, and she had just joined their ranks.

And that was enough. She didn't expect anything more from Sam. She had come to like and respect him, and she admitted to her reflection in the mirror, she *had* been attracted to him from the first. She just hadn't realized how much. But if this was all there was, it was more than enough. She had just had her first real eye-crossing orgasm!

Never one to run and hide, Naomi had always faced up to what she had done or what had been done to her, dealt with it, and moved on. She knew from her parents you could let life destroy you or you could fight the odds. She was the child of survivors, and she, too, had learned to survive. Certainly not the horrors her parents had faced, but she had her own demons. *And the blood-sucking lawyer.* She would deal with Sam in the morning. For now, she was going to savor her first few moments of genuine passion.

Stripping off her clothes, she quickly showered and then pulled on the nightshirt hanging on the bathroom door. She rinsed out the white bra and panties she had been wearing and hung them up with the other lingerie. After brushing her teeth, she winked at her reflection, and turned off the light. She was going to sleep *really good* tonight.

CHAPTER SIX

Sam was suffering the tortures of the damned. For all the screwing around he done during his years on the road, he still had a very active conscience.

I should not have gotten in her face, and I damn sure should not have gotten in her pants. Jesus. What was I thinking? I wasn't thinking, I was just wanting. It's been a damn long time since I've wanted a woman. Not since Beckie. Three damn long years.

A sob escaped Sam's throat. It echoed in the quiet of his room. It had been a little more than three years since his wife and daughter had died. He didn't even remember the first year, at least not much of it. His return to the human race had been forced upon him by Tommy and Tyrone. The pain had almost broken him…again. He had frozen up inside to protect what was left of his heart. On the outside, he looked like the old Sam, but on the inside, he had nothing left, except for his few close friends. Certainly nothing for another woman. *Three strikes and you're out.*

God damn it. Of course, it would be the way of things that when I finally feel something again, it would be for a smart-mouthed, pushy reporter, for Chrissake! I have totally fucked it up this time. She could write anything and it will sound shitty, just totally shitty.

Sam stopped himself on that thought, shaking his head, knowing Naomi would not compromise the story and his band just because he had taken advantage of her. He was used to women falling for him. *But, no, Naomi is not some star-struck groupie.* She had been around a lot of hot male singers and musicians and he could not remember hearing anything untoward about her. *No, everyone agrees she is a tough but fair journalist.* She had not fallen into his hands because he was a star. She had been awkward at first, almost like she was inexperienced. *Hell, how long had she been married? Maybe it has been a long stretch of celibacy for her, too.*

There had been a lot of women in his almost twenty years on the road but not nearly as many as some people imagined, and certainly not as many as some of his colleagues in the music business. There had been too many nights of rushing back onto the tour bus to get to the next gig, too many nights of bone-deep weariness, and too many nights when he had wanted to be alone— a melody playing in his head, just waiting for him to get it down on paper or play into a tape recorder. He blamed himself for his two failed marriages, but not because he had been unfaithful. He just had not been committed enough to Emily and Lola. *Damn, I was not committed enough to Beckie, either, or I would not have been on the road while she was home alone and pregnant, with a toddler. Damn me to Hell and back for that.*

Sam cursed himself again for being a fool. *Idiot.* Sex with Naomi had been fast and furious. *I took her standing up in a bathroom. Jesus, no finesse, no care. I didn't even stop long enough to use a rubber. And I left marks on her. My fingerprints are embedded on her hip. And probably other places, too. What an animal.* It flew in the face of his inbred respect for women that he had been rough with Naomi. He lay in the dark reliving his time with Naomi, cursing himself again as he tossed and turned, fighting off the images that had his cock hardening at the memory of her soft, slick warmth.

Dawn had just broken when Sam threw back the covers with a curse. *Fuck. If I can't sleep, I might as well run.* Stretching, he reached for his baggy cotton shorts, white socks, and running shoes. He pulled an old Oklahoma sweatshirt over his head, grabbed his baseball cap, sunglasses and room key, and headed out the door. Whenever Sam had the time on tour, he went for a run, usually in the early morning, but sometimes late at night. He nodded to the doorman and jogged across the street, heading for the park by the lake, where he knew he would find running paths and some solitude. The air smelled clean, and he had a lot to work out. A good long run would help clear his head.

An hour later, Sam came jogging back across the street, sweaty but no closer to a solution to his problem with Naomi. He headed into Drake Bros' to get a cup of coffee, but his steps slowed as he saw Tyrone at a table near the window. Tyrone looked up as Sam approached and kicked out the chair opposite him. *I'm not ready for this*. Sam groaned inwardly.

"Hoss, you look like the east end of a west-bound horse. What the hell did you do to yourself?" Tyrone scowled as he pushed his empty plate away and reached for his coffee mug. "You ain't drinkin' again?"

"Women, not whiskey, Ty. Only women troubles." Sam sighed, sinking into the offered chair. "Just some orange juice, honey," he threw over his shoulder to the approaching waitress.

"Get this boy a decent breakfast, will you, darlin'?" Tyrone called out to her. "He'll have what I had.

"What happened, Sam? You didn't go out last night 'cause you were mad at Naomi, did you? I thought you went back to your room after you busted up the party."

"I didn't *bust up* any party. I just didn't want any trouble with Beau. You know how he gets when he's had too much tequila and there's a pretty woman around."

"Pretty woman? Hell, JoEllen is like a sister to him, he isn't going to mess with her. Oh!" Tyrone, grinned as realization dawned. "You mean Naomi."

"Yes, I mean Naomi. You'would think I committed some kind of crime just because I was trying to keep her from getting into a mess with Beau. But, did she thank me? No, she lit into me like a wet hen," Sam muttered, throwing his cap on the table and rubbing his hands through his damp hair, making it stand up in grey and black spikes.

"I didn't hear any yelling from my room."

"Well, we weren't in the hall when she started yelling, we were in her room." Sam was red-faced, just remembering.

"You went back to her room? What were you doing in her bedroom, yelling at her?"

"I wasn't yelling at her, she was yelling at me and we were in the bathroom." Sam protested the accusing look in Tyrone's eyes. He knew Tyrone had developed a soft spot for Naomi and had some misguided notion she was fragile and needed his protection. *Yeah, right.* She was about as fragile as a cactus, all prickly, ready to stab at a man with all those barbs. But, he remembered, like a cactus when you got inside her, she was soft and sleek and *wet*. Sam smiled.

"Damn it all to hell and back!" Tyrone exploded. Sam's head jerked up and eyes came back into focus on Tyrone's angry face. Tyrone hissed fiercely, because heads were starting to turn in their direction. "You had her, didn't you? Tell me you didn't mess with her. Just tell me you weren't that stupid."

"Tyrone, I don't know what happened. We were yelling at each other, then I put my hands on her"

"Good Christ, you didn't hit her..." Tyrone whispered in disbelief. Sam had sunk pretty low on occasion when he'd been drinking, but Tyrone would never believe Sam had raised a hand to a woman.

"No. *NO!*" Sam was leaning forward, exasperated, reaching for Tyrone's gnarled hand. "No, I didn't hit her, but it happened so fast and, Jesus, Tyrone, it's been three years, and I just couldn't control myself. I was too rough. I left marks on her."

"You better not have made her cry, Sam. Everything we been through, and I'll hit you *myself* if you made that little lady cry. She's had enough hurtin' in this life with that ex-husband of hers. She don't deserve anymore and certainly not from the likes of you."

"She wasn't crying when I left last night. I think, I do believe, she was smiling."

But, she couldn't have been, I left marks on her. Christ, I took her like a stallion in heat!

"I don't want to hear no more now, boy." Tyrone put his hands up. Just like the kids said, *too much information.* "Thank you, darlin'," he said when the waitress refilled his coffee cup after she had put Sam's plate in front of him.

"You better make sure everything is right with her before tonight, Sam. We've got a show to do, and you don't need any distractions now. I know you, you'll get all moody if you worry this thing. Get it right with her."

How the hell am I supposed to do that? Sam wondered for the tenth time later that morning. He had finished breakfast alone, posed for a picture with the waitress after she recognized him, and then gone upstairs to shower. He wanted to run over to the arena and check out the piano again. It just didn't sound right to him, and he was very particular about his piano—it was a Steinway baby grand, and it had traveled with Sam for the last five years.

Sam was just striding out of the elevator into the lobby when he saw Naomi. At least he thought it was Naomi, heading out of the hotel, just steps ahead of him. Calling her name, he ran to catch up with her. Naomi slowed her pace and turned. Sam skidded to a stop in front of her.

No words formed in his mouth because he was speechless at the sight of her. *That is a whole lot of woman.* Naomi had on a long black dress, clingy but not tight, hugging that gorgeous butt of hers and holding her beautiful breasts in its soft caress. The slit up to her knee showed her long legs, revealing her perfect calves. She wasn't wearing her trademark cowboy boots or those ridiculous turquoise moccasins she wandered around in sometimes, but some strappy black heels. The warming breeze started blowing her hair around her shoulders, and that's when Sam realized why he hadn't been sure it was her. Her hair was straight, pulled back from her face with a black clip. She wasn't wearing much makeup either. *Not that she needs* it, Sam thought. *She looks like she's had about ten hours of sleep, with nothing but sweet dreams.*

"What did you do to your hair?" was the first thing out of his mouth. His eyes skimmed over her, looking for any other signs of his abuse. His cheeks reddened as he thought of the bruises on her hip.

"I blew it out this morning after my shower. Takes forever, but I like it to be a little less…um, flamboyant when I go to *shul*. I mean, services."

"You're going to church?" Sam was confused. "After last night?"

Naomi's eyes flared, and Sam had the grace to look embarrassed. "I mean, I thought you'd sleep in this morning."

"Oh. Good. I'm glad you weren't trying to imply that a sinner such as myself had no business worshiping with decent people. I'd have to call you a hypocrite," she snapped. He snuck off to church himself when he had some time and could find a Southern Baptist church to his liking—one with lots of singing.

"Hell, Naomi, you know that's not what I meant. It's Saturday…." Sam felt somewhat abashed, especially since he was getting uncomfortably hard just standing close to her. When she was angry, her chest heaved, by God it did, and he couldn't take his eyes off her.

"Jews go to services on Saturday morning. It's the Sabbath. I am a Jew so I'm going to services," she explained, patiently. He hoped the woman would take pity on him, he was so uncomfortable around her, ashamed and aroused all at the same time. "Look, when I get the chance, and I can find a synagogue near where I'm staying, I like to visit them when I'm traveling. Makes me feel connected and, sometimes, I just need the peace. There's a nice Reform temple just around the corner. I found it last time I was here, so I thought since we were staying over, I'd go to services. It's no big deal."

"Can I walk with you? We need to talk." Sam took her arm and then stopped. The heat that flashed through him just by touching her stunned him. She felt it too, he could tell by the faint tremor that rippled through her. *What the hell is this?*

"Naomi, I'm sorry about last night." She started to speak, so he rushed on. "I'm not sorry that we made love, but I'm so sorry that I hurt you. You have every right to be disgusted. I lost control, and I was too rough with you." He was starting to choke on the words, the bile rising in his throat at his fierce treatment of her, but he had to get it out. "I left marks on you. I never would have believed I could do such a thing if I hadn't seen the bruises on your hip. And I didn't use any protection, either." He cast her a sidelong glance and stuttered to a stop. She had that *shit-eating* grin again, like last night.

"Well, you're in for a surprise. Look at this one!" she laughed, as she pulled the neckline of her dress down to reveal a hickey near her collarbone. "Sam," she said gently, curling her hand around his neck and pulling him a little closer so he could hear her whispered words, "I have never been *fucked* like that before in my life!" His mouth dropped open.

"Jesus, Naomi, do you kiss your mother with that mouth?"

"Yup." Naomi grinned. "And I pray with it too and sing in the shower and drink tequila, and I even kiss randy country singers with it!

"Sam, Sam. Do you know what it does to a thirty-six year old woman with a twelve-year old son, some stretch marks, and a few well-concealed grey hairs to be wanted so badly by a man that his hands shake? Your desire for me was the best aphrodisiac in the world. You lost control? You made me lose control! Me! I am the biggest control freak in the world, and I would have done anything you wanted me to last night just to get closer to your fire, just to see if you could make me burn the way you were burning. And you did. I swear to you, I had only read about orgasms like that. I'm not sorry about anything we did. We're grown-ups, we're not responsible to anyone, and we've paid our dues. The kind of sex we had doesn't happen to everyone, it's pretty rare from what I've heard. And I will never forget it. As for protection, I'm on the pill. I need it to regulate my periods." She reached up to kiss his chin chastely. "Now, can I go to services and repent, just in case...?"

Sam stood staring at her. This woman was something—he wasn't sure what—but he knew he wanted to find out more about her. She was a bundle of contradictions. He had just scratched the surface of all that was Naomi. And he wanted her again, now and later.

"Come on," he said, tucking her hand in the crook of his arm, "I'll walk you."

After Naomi disappeared inside the synagogue, Sam went on to the arena, but he couldn't concentrate on the piano or anything else except Naomi. He wandered back toward where he'd left her, hoping to bump into her, but when he got there, it was obvious the services had not yet finished. He could hear singing through the open front doors, a haunting melody that tugged at him and started him to thinking, but his thoughts were as fragmented as the bits of music he heard. Nonetheless, he was humming the unknown song as he walked back to the hotel. *It just might work, if he could only find the words.*

Thank God the words to the service were universal and well-known to Naomi. Her mind was definitely not on the prayers being recited in the cool confines of the synagogue. Try as she might to concentrate on the present, all she could think about was the past— last night and this morning.

She had slept the sleep of the blessed and awakened rested but restless. A few stretches loosened most of the kinks from sleeping on a firm hotel mattress, but her first steps upon rising revealed how well Sam had used her. *Haha. I'm feeling sore in places I didn't even know I had muscles.* The tremors in her inner thighs, the ache deep within her pelvis, and a slight kink in her lower back had her smiling as she showered.

She had planned to attend services even before her encounter with Sam, but Naomi felt the need for spiritual connection even more as she contemplated the consequences of their coming together, while she dried her hair and got dressed.

The sound of his voice as she left the hotel sent a shiver of dread down her back and a jolt of desire straight to her vagina.

God, he is gorgeous! Naomi thought when he approached her. Sam's looks always caught her by surprise. Maybe not gorgeous in the classic sense, but he was so male, so hard and so sexy. He had a way of looking at you with those ice blue eyes, as if he was looking out from under the brim of a hat—which he usually was. And those thick, curly black eyelashes. His eyes alone made the breath catch in her throat. He almost always wore a black cowboy hat onstage, with washed-out T-shirts or worn denim shirts that set off his eyes. But this morning, he was wearing a white T-shirt, faded blue jeans, and Docksiders, his head bare. He looked like he had stepped out of *GQ*'s weekend grunge issue.

She shook her head and tried again to focus on the service. Good thing she had found a seat in the back of the sanctuary. Her face was warm so she knew she was blushing as she remembered Sam's sweet and totally unnecessary apology. Her fingers rubbed against her hip, finding the sensitive spot where his fingers had bruised her while he held her hard against him.

Naomi had not been able to find the words last night or this morning, but she needed to let him know what he had done for her. She had been pretty badly hurt by her husband, emotionally more than physically, and her self-confidence as a woman had been shattered by his words and actions. If nothing else, she was grateful to Sam for showing her she was a desirable woman. It was a gift she would always treasure, even though she was sure he would not understand…he who had been sought after by hundreds of women over the years, and had been caught by dozens of them.

As the Torah service began, Naomi rose with the rest of the congregation. Pulled back into the present by the traditional words and melodies, she thanked God for the many blessings in her life and prayed she would find a way to make sense of everything that had happened. Then with a heartfelt sigh, she lost herself in the ancient words of Moses.

CHAPTER SEVEN

"Where's Naomi?" Sam asked no one in particular. The backstage area was crowded with guests, crew, the band, and assorted hangers-on. Naomi had not returned to the Drake before he left for the United Center. When he got there, Tyrone told him she, Bobbi and JoEllen had gone shopping at some mall. Bobbi and JoEllen had shown up later in the afternoon, but Naomi had not been with them.

"She was talking to her kid on the phone when we left the hotel. He was giving her a hard time. But she said she'd be along directly," Tyrone answered him, in between bites into another chicken wing. Sam had never been able to figure out how Tyrone could eat greasy, spicy, hot wings before a performance. Sam always felt like he was going to throw up before he went on stage, so he kept his pre-show meals light and bland.

"She's over by the extra amplifiers talking to that DJ fellow who was warming up the crowd," Chase commented as he walked by with his guitar in one arm and his other arm around a tall redhead in skin-tight denim.

Sam looked in the direction Chase pointed. Naomi's blonde mane was bobbing emphatically as the DJ leaned down to her, speaking rapidly. Sam was moving toward her when he felt a hand on his shoulder. He spun around.

"Jackson! Good to see you, boy. You ready?"

"Yeah, I'm all set. I'll come out, like we rehearsed, on the third song to take over the piano when you start on the guitar. Then, when you get to "The Roadie Song", the light will come up on the second verse. Hey, is that Naomi Stein over there?" Jackson Browne nodded his head in Naomi's direction.

"You know her?" Sam asked, none too politely.

"Met her a few years ago in LA. She's something, isn't she?" Jackson said as he hurried over to Naomi. Sam sucked in his breath as he saw him touch her back. She turned, then let out a squeal and launched herself into Jackson Browne's arms. *Good Christ! Did the woman know every man in the business?*

Naomi was hugging the singer as though he was her long lost friend. *And what the hell did she have on?* Gone were the black jeans and the black leather jacket, but not the red cowboy boots. She was wearing a red sundress, with wide straps and white lace peeking out from the tight band above her breasts and just below the long full skirt. She had thrown on a faded denim jacket and lots of silver bracelets. She looked like a country girl, except for the flame red nails and lipstick. Her carmined mouth had left its mark on Jackson's cheek, but he didn't seem to mind. The two had their heads together, laughing intimately. Sam felt his anger rise. His anger, and something else. Tyrone had come to stand next to him. He nudged Sam none too gently with his gnarled finger.

"You better suck it in, Hoss. We've got a show to do in about fifteen minutes, and you need to get your head straight. There's nothing going on over there. And it's not like you have any cause to say anything about it even if there was. That girl might be wearing your brand..." Sam's head whipped around as he glared at Tyrone. "Yup. I seen your mark on her. But, she's all grown up, and she can do as she pleases. You have no call to get a mad on because she's flirting with an old friend. And that's all he is to her."

"She's acting like he's a lot more than an old friend," Sam muttered.

"You jealous, Hoss?" Tyrone asked softly.

"No. She just shouldn't be throwing herself at every man who comes along."

Tyrone laughed. "Well, son, you should know all about women throwing themselves at a man. You got your fair share over the years, and I don't recollect as how you threw too many back."

"That was different." Even as he said it, Sam realized how childish he sounded. He felt so possessive of Naomi, and she had such an immediate effect on him each time he saw her. He had been walking around all day almost completely hard after his morning encounter with her. His undisciplined appendage had been under some control, until he saw her in Jackson's arms.

"C'mon, boy. Time to get ready." Tyrone pulled him toward the stage door. "Hey, everybody, its time," he called out to Mickey, Beau, Chase, JoEllen, and Bobbi. Tommy motioned them over, all the while keeping up his continuous stream of directions to the crew through his headset.

They joined in a circle, held hands, and asked God's blessing on their work for that night. "God bless us and keep us and guide us and let us bring some happiness to those who have come to hear us and some relief to those who will benefit from this concert. Thank you, Lord, for giving us the ability to make music and for bringing out the people. Amen."

Naomi stood quietly outside the circle. It was almost the same prayer every night, but it always got to her. Many of the performers she had toured with offered a prayer before going on stage, but something in Sam's simple plea touched her deeply. He obviously had deep faith and a strong sense of charity. For this tour, at Sam's instruction, Tommy had made sure the tickets sold at reasonable prices so everyone had a chance to see the show. And Naomi discovered Sam's portion of the proceeds in each city were donated to a local charity as his way of giving back. He was turning out to be a much more complex man than she had realized. *Aren't they all?*

Standing in the shadows off stage, Naomi was transfixed again for over two hours as Sam played to the enthusiastic audience. The song sets were similar in every show, but Sam tailored his remarks to each city's audience. Every show opened with a video shot from the bus as it entered each city. Naomi knew the crew shot additional footage during the day of different landmarks and attractions that would be familiar to the audience. The video played on the big screen in lieu of a warm-up act, to the soundtrack of Sam's duet with Willie Nelson on Willie's trademark "On the Road Again." The crowd roared as shots of Navy Pier, Ebbets Field and Lake Michigan flashed on the screen.

She felt herself being caught up in the magic that surrounded this tour. It wasn't the music, it wasn't the guest performers, it wasn't even the idea of the mystery guest, as Jed had thought.

There was something else going on between Sam and his fans. Naomi's mind could not quite place it yet, but it was almost as if Sam's fans sensed how close they had come to losing him and were trying to let him know how relieved and thankful they were to have him back. For Sam, there seemed to be a need to acknowledge his fans had filled the gaping hole left in his life by the loss of his family. *No, that's not it.* Not that the fans could make up for Sam's loss, more like the music had given him something to live for.

Hours later, after the show, two encores, and the party in the dressing rooms, Naomi went backstage to pick up her Prada tote bag. She was looking for the door to the parking lot when she heard piano notes, tentative and soft—but strangely familiar. She turned toward the stage, feeling her way. Most of the lights were out. The roadies would finish loading in the morning. There was a faint glow from the stage and the music was louder. *What is that? I know that song.* Then it came to her, as she walked out onto the stage and saw Sam bathed in the light of the single lamp burning on his baby grand. He was playing "Mi Kamocha" or at least, fragments of it. He was frowning as he found the notes on the piano. And, he seemed so alone.

"Sam," she called to him quietly. "Are you all right? What are you playing?"

He turned to her, his arm resting on the piano's glossy black surface.

"It's something I heard today when I was out walking around." He seemed embarrassed by his answer. "Hey, what are you doing here? I thought you left with Jackson."

"That sounded like an accusation, not a question, Sam. Jackson left with some of the radio people."

"Oh. I thought, you know, since you seemed to know each other so well you might want to leave with him."

"I've known him a long time, Sam, but not in the Biblical sense, if that's what you were hinting at." She walked out of the light and into the shadows surrounding the piano. Her bag plopped on the floor heavily as she came to lean against the piano, just inches away from him.

"Are you jealous?" Naomi asked. She really didn't need this from Sam. Her ex-husband had been jealous and suspicious, and all the while, he was the one screwing around. *Men.*

"No, I'm not jealous. I just know him, too, and he has a reputation and...."

Sam broke off, his fingers idly strumming over the keyboard.

"You have a reputation, too, you know, Sam."

"Not for a long time." He said it softly, looking up at her with those blue eyes, shining through his impossibly thick black lashes. Naomi's heart melted a little and a sigh escaped her. She smiled at his transparent attempt to get to her. It was working.

"Don't question me, okay? I got enough of that from the blood-sucking lawyer."

"The blood-sucking lawyer you were married to?"

"The very same. He could turn a simple conversation into a cross-examination in minutes. God, I hated that about him. I never knew when he was going to go off on his district attorney routine. He only worked there one summer—not enough money in public service. He found the pot of gold in trusts and estates. And divorces. Especially ours." Naomi sounded bitter. And she was. Not so much for herself, although he had done a lot of damage to her self-esteem. It was mostly what he had done to Jonah.

"So, why did you and your husband break up?" Sam leaned toward her as he softly asked the question.

"It's the same old story, nothing you'd be interested in." Naomi did not want to talk about her ex-husband with Sam. It would give him too much information.

"I'll bet it's *not* the same old story. I can't figure it out. It couldn't have been that you were fooling around—you're too decent for that. You're smart and funny and caring and beautiful. After last night, I know it couldn't have been the sex, so what was it?"

"It *was* the sex." *Why did I blurt that out?* She hoped he could not see her flaming cheeks in the half-light of the stage.

"That's not funny." Sam looked up at her face. "You mean it, it really was the sex?"

"I really don't want to talk about it," she replied, stiffly. *Just leave it alone, Sam,* she pleaded silently. Thinking about the debacle her marriage had become was the surest way to ruin what had been a beautiful day, and what promised to be an equally wonderful evening.

"Darlin', it couldn't have been you. You're about the sexiest woman I've ever been with. You made me go off like some green kid."

Blushing, Naomi murmured, "It was never like that for me before, Sam. You were the first to make me feel that way. It was overwhelming. It was like it wasn't me."

Sam thought he was going to get her to tell him the whole story of the blood-sucking lawyer, but not tonight. Naomi looked so vulnerable standing there, in her ridiculously innocent, but sexy, sundress. He pulled her toward him then, pulled her between his legs, so her bottom plunked down on the piano keys. She jumped, but he settled her again, firmly in front of him. Sam didn't want to touch her, he didn't want to hurt her again, but she looked so sad.

He tilted her chin up; he could see the tears blurring those beautiful eyes. His thumbs skimmed up to wipe the tears away from the corners. He took her trembling hands in his. Then he leaned forward, resting his forehead on their clasped hands. Her scent filled his head, the spicy fragrance she wore, the hot, woman scent of her. He hardened even more. *The woman can make me hard just with her smell.* His tongue stroked her fingers, slipping between them, sucking lightly on the tips. Naomi moaned softly, and the sound moved him immeasurably.

Sam looked up at Naomi, their eyes met and locked. His hands reached up to slip her denim jacket off those soft, strong shoulders. He swore softly when he saw the mark on her shoulder, partially hidden by the strap of her sundress. The calloused tip of his finger traced the mark, then dipped under the strap, following it down to the soft swell of her breast. Her hand stopped his exploration.

"Sam, is this a good idea? I mean, aren't there people around? What if someone sees us?" she stammered uncomfortably.

"No, the guys know to leave me alone if I head back to the stage afterward. They'll be in tomorrow morning to load up. It's okay."

It was as if he drew a line of fire on her skin. Naomi's eyes followed the path of Sam's finger, until her involuntary inrush of breath as she watched his fingers dipping into the neckline of the dress. Her eyes darted to his face. He smiled his slow, seductive smile as both hands fastened on the first, then the second, then the third button that held the tight bodice closed. They slipped, as if by their own volition, from the buttonholes.

"What have we here?" he asked slyly, as his hands parted the front of her dress to reveal a lacy red demi-bra. He sat upright. "Jesus, did you all find a Frederick's of Hollywood at the mall? Don't even tell me Bobbi and JoEllen bought any of this stuff—I don't want to know." The spidery red fabric barely contained her breasts. He sucked his breath in, almost afraid of what he would unveil next.

Naomi laughed, shakily "Well, JoEllen was looking at a black lace thong, and Bobbi bought this strapless…" She stopped when he laid his hands on her breasts, just resting there. Her skin warmed to his touch, as though his fingers were rays of hot Tulsa sun on her skin. Then his fingers reached for the buttons again.

She trembled as he slipped each button slipped from its mooring. He felt the tension in her and each tiny quiver as his fingers loosened her dress. She leaned into him, resting her forehead on the top of his head.

"I love the smell of your hair. You smell like a forest after the rain, the pine scent of your shampoo cuts through the stale smell here." She lifted her head to smile down at him. "You have the best hair, soft and springy, with some curl. The light from the lamp turns those few strands of grey to silver."

Her words were lost in Sam's exclamation. "Done. Let's just see what we have here." *Dear Jesus God*! He had drawn her dress apart to find only a whisper of red lace between her thighs. He groaned. *She's killing me!*

His arms went around her, holding her tightly, pressing her warm flesh into the soft denim covering his hardness. He leaned in to kiss her, moaning into her mouth. He kissed her with all the longing in his heart and all the loneliness of the last three years. "This is not going to work." Sam said it more to himself than to Naomi. He stood in a rush and lifted her onto the piano top. *What am I going to do with this woman?*

Naomi was overwhelmed with strange new sensations; her arms wrapped as tightly around his neck as his were around her waist. She felt like she was drowning, and he was all that she could hold onto in the turbulent sea of feelings that was swirling around her. The passion had flared between them so fast and so hot she was unprepared for the onslaught of wanting that swept through her. With all his protestations earlier in the day, she had not been certain they would be together again, and she had thought she was fine. But now that she was in his arms and his mouth was on hers, she didn't know if she would ever be able to let him go.

"Naomi. God help me, I want you so bad." Sam's hands were in her hair, and he rained kisses over her face, telling her with his tender licks and bites just how much he wanted her. His mouth was like a hot brand on her neck, but then he stopped and tenderly kissed the mark he had left on her shoulder.

She twisted in his arms now, trying to pull his mouth back to hers, and he complied. His tongue sank into the deep recesses of her mouth. Naomi caught him gently with her teeth and sucked on his tongue as if she wanted to draw him even further inside of her.

It was Sam who broke the kiss, pulling her face to his shoulder, while he gasped for breath. "Woman, you're going to be the death of me." His laugh was shaky and his hands trembled as they swept into the folds of her dress. Naomi's back arched as his hands found her bare skin. The man's fingers worked magic on his piano's keyboard and the strings of his guitar, but nothing like the magic she felt when his calloused fingertips played across her ribcage.

"I've been wanting to do this all day, ever since I saw you dressed so chaste and sweet for services. I haven't been able to get these beautiful breasts out of my mind, and I haven't even really seen them yet. But, now, I will."

His fingers unclasped the front closure on her bra and his hands freed her from its clinging confines. Sam bent to her, kissing her breasts, her chest, her collarbone. It was sweet but not what she wanted and not what she needed, desperately. "Sam, please, please."

Those pleas ended in a gasp when his mouth found a nipple. While his hand played with her other nipple, plucking and shaping her, his tongue laved the hard crest before he drew her into his mouth. Naomi had to put her hands on the piano's smooth surface for support. Her head fell back as streamers of pure pleasure shot through her. His voice, harsh in the silence of the arena, caused her to look back up at him.

"Darlin'. Look at yourself." His fingers trailed a line from her face down to her breasts. "That long clean line of your throat, the way your collarbone breaks that smooth stretch of skin until the swell of your breasts curve out from your body. *There is nothing as beautiful as that line.* God, you're like some Michelangelo sculpture." She felt a flush creep up her torso at his admiring words. But before she could speak, he turned his attention to her other nipple.

When it was as wet and red as its twin from his ministrations, he continued his trail of kisses across her belly to the edge of red lace. His tongue dipped below the confines of fabric to the curls beneath. She could feel the warmth of his breath on her belly and thighs as he sat down. He buried his face between her legs, his hands sloping down to cup her buttocks.

"Sweet, sweet," he murmured. He pushed the scrap of lace aside with his tongue.

"Oh God, oh God," was all she could say, her head shaking back and forth, swirling her long hair across the piano, not believing, not quite hoping, that he was going to caress her in a way that she had never experienced, but that she now desperately desired.

"You're so wet, Naomi. You get so wet for me, darlin'. It's so sweet, like honey." His mouth was hot against the last strip of fabric separating them from their desires. And then it was gone and his mouth was on her. His tongue probed between the soft folds of flesh and she found her legs opening to give him the freedom he sought, her hips arching to meet him. In seconds, he had her whimpering and moving against his mouth, her small nub of pleasure receiving licks and nips from him. He buried his face in her curls, his tongue flicking at her. Then his tongue was sliding into her. It was beyond her imagination; nothing had prepared her for these sensations. She could hear him, the sounds that his mouth made on her as he ate at her delicate flesh. He was moaning. She felt herself starting to lose control and she could tell he felt it too. Her skin was flushed, her nipples hard and thrusting and the flesh on her thighs rippled as she strove to retain control over the flood of feelings emanating from his mouth.

"Come, Naomi. Come in my mouth. Baby, baby, please," he crooned to her. She may have been able to hold on but for his hot words and his fingers slipping inside her just as he took her throbbing bud into his mouth and sucked. She could not have stopped then if she had wanted to—and she didn't want to. The orgasm shaking her, she came and came, and still his mouth was on her, pushing her into another climax before the first ended. Falling back on the piano, clutching the bunched fabric of her dress as she reached for something, anything to hold onto, before she fell into the abyss of desire again.

Naomi was whimpering when Sam stood and pulled her up into his arms. She felt as limp as a rag doll. "There now," he stroked her hair and whispered. "There now, that was better, wasn't it? No bruises?"

Looking up at him through barely opened eyes, she said, "That was unbelievable."

Sam's lips were red, still wet from her. She couldn't believe it when her insides tightened again, just from looking at him, knowing what he had just done to her. She didn't think he could have aroused her anymore but he did, just standing there. Naomi leaned up and licked at his lips, tasting herself on him, tasting the fruits of their passion.

His whole body shook at her bold move. "Stop, darlin', stop, or I'll take you right here on this piano. I swear, I will."

"Good." She slid down to the keyboard; her hands reached for his belt buckle. He was hard and straining against his jeans.

"Naomi, by God, don't do that or..." He stopped on a gasp as her hands freed him from the constraints of denim and cotton. She stroked his hard length, her thumb spreading the drop of desire that had already escaped his control over the smooth head of his penis.

Need made her bold. Her voice had dropped an octave. "You'll what, Cowboy? You'll take me? How about if I take you?" Drawing him toward her, the tip of his desire grazed her wet heat. He shook as he reached for her hips, lifting her toward him. She guided him into her depths, where she was already starting to spasm again.

"Is this what you want? Is this it?" he growled as he thrust into her, burying himself deep inside her. Her silent response was to wrap her legs around his waist and her arms around his shoulders. Lifting her hips, he slid home.

His climax exploded in her, never-ending, while her inner muscles clenched around him like a velvet fist, milking him of every drop of his passion. And she whispered over and over, "Yes.

Yes. Yes, Sam," until there was no sound between them except for her sighs and the beating of his heart.

CHAPTER EIGHT

Lola Hogan Rhodes showed up at the concert in Bozeman, Montana. Her arrival at one of the tour's venues had been expected by everyone, except Sam and Naomi. The only question for the band and crew had been *when*. Naomi had heard some of the roadies placing bets on which city was likely to be the site of Lola's *command performance*. No one had placed any bets on Bozeman and The Brick Breeden Fieldhouse at Montana State University, a concert site with more sentimental than commercial value to Sam and his original band mates. The sound check had been progressing through the afternoon. Naomi was sitting with the sound technicians and Tommy. Suddenly Tommy threw his headset against the console and swore.

"God damn it to hell and back. *Just* what I need today!"

With a quizzical look on her face, Naomi glanced up from her laptop where she was making notes about the vast technical requirements of Sam's tour. One of the sound guys asked Tommy, "You okay, boss?"

"No, I'm screwed is what I am! Lola just pulled up backstage. I'm going to try to head her off before she gets to Sam." He rushed down the aisle and out to the curtained area next to the stage.

"What's going on?" Naomi asked Bob, the sound technician, as she packed up her laptop.

"Well, Lola likes to cause trouble, and Sam just doesn't see it. She usually gets everybody pissed off about something. It's not so bad if it's after a show, but before..." His voice trailed off and he just shrugged.

"So, she's a real *kokh leffel*, pot-stirrer, is she?" Naomi murmured more to herself than to Bob, who just shook his head and turned back to the soundboard.

Naomi headed backstage herself. Maybe she would finally get some information about the mysterious Lola. Sam and Tyrone were at the piano with John Mellencamp, the evening's surprise guest. They had just finished a rousing rendition of "Jack and Diane", and now they were working on one of Sam's old songs, "Promise Me." JoEllen and Bobbi were off to the side, singing quietly, heads bent together. Naomi moved toward them just as they looked up and frowned at the unfolding drama by the stage door.

Tommy was engaged in a heated conversation with Lola and a platinum blonde, thin, young man dressed in a Western-style suit. Sam's second wife was something to see. She was tall and had a long auburn mane, artfully curled and arranged. Her lean figure was tanned and toned and adorned with diamonds at every conceivable point. Her well cut white dress and jacket showed her body to perfection. She exuded expensive glamour and something else. Malevolence, Naomi thought.

"She always wore white to Sam's black. I think she thought it made her look virginal. I always thought it made her look emotionless, like a dead person in a shroud." Bobbi murmured in Naomi's ear. Naomi chuckled at Bobbi's wry description.

"Why doesn't Tommy want Sam to see her?" Naomi queried Sam's cousin.

"Well, she went back sniffing around Sam after Beckie died. She wanted to do a duet album with him, but Tommy and Tyrone kept her away from Sam. Tommy never liked Lola; he could see what she was after. Sam doesn't even know she ever was at the Colorado place." Bobbi's lips pressed in a hard line as she finished.

"And what was she after?"

Bobbi sighed and said, "You're going to hear it from someone today. It might as well be me. Lola wanted to be a star, a big star, with Hollywood movies and TV specials and platinum albums. Sam just wanted to sing his songs to the people, write songs for other singers, and play guitar with the guys—just make music, you understand. She pushed him and pushed him. He tried to appease her for a while, but when she found out he'd given away a song to Garth Brooks and Trisha Yearwood, Lola lost it completely. That's when she left him, right in the middle of a tour. And she was pretty cold about it. Didn't let anyone know; Sam was frantic with worry. We found out about it from the local radio station. Lola said some things to the papers and to some disc jockeys. She left a bad taste in everyone's mouth. Except Sam. He always makes excuses for her, said he owed her for keeping him going after he and Emily broke up. There's some who will say Lola found her way into Sam's bed before he and Emily officially separated, but you can't prove it by me."

Sam turned toward the rising voices. He paused when he saw Lola. Naomi could have sworn his shoulders slumped imperceptibly before he straightened them. He rose and moved past the women to where Lola and Tommy still argued.

"Hello, sweet thing. You never change. You look like a million dollars. Come here and give me a kiss and leave Tommy alone. I swear, you two are always at each other." Sam was already reaching for the redhead, when she squealed "Sammy" and threw herself into his arms.

"*Sammy*? Hell, that alone would be enough to make me hate her." Naomi said sarcastically to Bobbi.

"Damn, I like you, Naomi!" Bobbi slung her arm across Naomi's shoulders as the two stood and watched the scene play out before their eyes. Sam positioned himself between Lola and Tommy; Lola's escort hovered around trying to look useful. Within a few moments, Sam was taking Lola by the hand and leading her to the stage. Tommy just shook his head, muttered a few foul words, and headed back to the sound check. The blond young man went back to the limousine. That was the last Naomi saw of any of them until just before Sam and Lola went on stage.

It pained her to admit it to herself later that night, but *the woman certainly could sing*. Naomi was in her room at the rustic inn after the show, sending an e-mail to Jonah in response to yet another plea to take him out of that *damn hellhole* she had stuck him in. Rubbing the sharp pain blooming between her eyes, Naomi wished for Sam. But he was off again with Lola. For some reason, that pissed her off more than Jonah's scathing e-mail.

Well, it's none of my damn business what he does. She fumed silently. Sam had climbed into Lola's white limousine right after the show, as big as life and twice as handsome, never even looking at Naomi or anyone else for that matter.

Jesus, can't the man see what a conniving bloodsucker the flashy redhead is? She really can sing, though. Lola had done a lovely rendition of "There is Someone Walking Behind You". And she and Sam had brought the house down with the haunting "In Another's Eyes", the song he had given to Garth and Trisha.

The lid on her laptop had just been clicked shut when Naomi heard a light rap on her door. She opened it immediately, and there was Sam, hat in hand, sheepish grin on his face. "I didn't know if you'd still be up, we leave so early tomorrow.... Can I come in?"

Naomi stepped aside so he could enter the room. As he brushed by her, she caught the aroma of heavy, expensive perfume. Lola's perfume. Her nostrils and then her temper flared.

"Where have you been, Sam? A quick one in the back of the limo for old time's sake?" *Where had that come from?*

His eyes flashed blue lightening as he spun around to face her. "What do you mean by that crack? I just rode with Lola to the airport. We had some business to discuss."

"I thought you two didn't do business anymore, Sam. Or was it personal business?"

"I don't have to put up with your bullshit, Naomi. You don't need to know every damn bit of my life for your damn article. Jesus, where do you people draw the line?"

"What do you mean, *you people*? Do you mean reporters? Or just women who you've screwed?"

"That's enough, God damn it! You know what I mean. You push too much sometimes, Naomi. Just let it lie. Just let it lie for once." Sam was twisting his old baseball cap in his hands, his face hard and his eyes cold.

"Oh, be a good little girl and let the man handle his affairs himself and keep my nose out of it? Not damn likely, Cowboy!" She was in a rage now. There was no way in Hell she was going to lay down so a man could walk all over her. *Again.*

"Fine, then. I'm out of here. I don't need this crap from you, *sweetheart!*" Sam turned and grabbed the doorknob, wrenching the door open violently.

"Don't let it hit you in the ass as you walk out, *darlin'!*" She slammed the door so hard the noise reverberated in the silence left in Sam's wake. The silence soon broken by Naomi's sobs.

Naomi knocked several time on the door to Sam's room. She heard his feet hit the floor amidst his muffled curses. He sounded like he was still pissed off. *Maybe this is not such a good idea.* She heard the rustle of his jeans as he approached the door.

He cursed again then barked, "This better be good."

Sam got to the door just as Naomi was turning away. She was wearing a grey hooded sweatshirt thrown over the Winnie the Pooh nightshirt she sometimes wore.

"Get in here before someone sees you in that stupid outfit," Sam said as he pulled her into the room. He pushed the door shut behind her and stood glaring at her. She could see he was still angry at what he probably felt were intrusive questions.

"Sorry if I woke you up, Sam. But, I couldn't sleep knowing how angry you were with me. I came to say I'm sorry but that..." She stopped as he glared at her. His hands were rubbing through his hair, making it stand on end in black and silver curls. His stretching brought the muscles of his torso into stark relief in the light from the single lamp glowing softly in the room. Her eyes traced the mat of hair from his chest to where it became a narrow line of black curls snaking into the opening of his jeans, widening as she saw the transformation of his body taking place before her eyes. She licked her lips, her mouth suddenly gone dry.

Sam was watching her through narrowed eyes and groaned when her tongue slipped through her lips. At the sound of his desire, Naomi's gasped; her nipples felt like they were poking right through the thin pink material of her nightshirt. They stared at each other, motionless. Then Sam dragged her into his arms. His mouth came down hard on hers, forcing her lips to open. His tongue was inside her mouth, filling her, silencing her. His hands fisted in her hair, holding her so she couldn't move.

She didn't want to be anywhere other than where she was. *He didn't hate her.* Having so recently discovered his passion, Naomi had been bereft at the thought they might never be together again because of her persistent questioning. *It will be over between us soon enough, but not now, not yet.*

Sam lifted his mouth from hers. Her lips were already swollen from his kiss. He rested his chin on top of her tousled golden curls.

"Darlin', I just can't seem to keep my hands off you," he

whispered, holding her close.

"Sam. Sam, you have to let me explain."

"Let's not talk about it, Naomi," he spoke into her hair, her neck, her ear.

"No." She pushed away from him, leaning back against the door. "Listen to me. I'm only going to say this to you once. I wasn't questioning you about Lola for the article. What happens between us...um...uh...sexually, has nothing to do with us professionally. I won't write about you that way. I didn't want to know about Lola for the article. I wanted to know for me."

Sam's eyes widened at that last. "What does Lola have to do with you and me?" he asked. "It was over between us a long time ago."

"Sam, she still means something to you. And I was...jealous. She's so possessive about you. And you let her," Naomi finished accusingly.

Sam smiled sadly at Naomi. The smile said that she still didn't really know him.

"What else does she have, Naomi? She never remarried and you saw the guy she was with. Her career, as she refers to it, has gone well, certainly, but not as far as she wanted it to. My career is on fire, and it galls her because she knows it was something I never sought, never wanted. What harm is there in letting her believe she still has a small part of it? Who is hurt if she sings a few songs with me? The fans love it. I like it, too. We made pretty good music together for a while, and she was good to me, in her way. She left feeling good about herself, and it cost me nothing to give that to her." He shrugged. Then he smiled that *Sam* smile at her. "So, you were jealous? About what?"

Naomi had the grace to blush. "Let's just say, I was worried you'd have no tonsils left after that parting kiss on stage. Who knew what would happen in the limo?"

"Honey, you've had that acerbic tongue of yours a lot further down my throat than she did. You could have slit my throat from the inside." He chuckled at her look of outrage.

"Thanks a lot, Sam. That's the last time I ever apologize to you, you ungrateful philistine." Naomi turned and reached for the doorknob. Sam was on her in an instant, his hard body pressing into hers, his hands on either side of her head.

"Oh, no, New York," he growled. "You come down here, wake me up, and then expect to walk away and leave me with nothing but the image of you and Winnie the Pooh? I don't think so." He leaned into her, fitting his erection between the curves of her bottom.

"What do you want, Cowboy?" Naomi turned in his arms. "Feel like getting your throat slit?" Her eyes drifted down the front of him to where his cock had already grown above the zipper of his jeans. *God, he's so hard and so big. Do I do that to him?* A tantalizing thought came to her then. *Do I have the nerve?*

"Or maybe something else needs the feel of my, what did you so charmingly call it, *acerbic tongue*?"

Her hands reached out to cup him. He was like a rock and throbbed at her touch. Naomi could feel her nipples hardening and she could feel his hot gaze on them. Pulling his zipper down carefully, she freed him from his denim constraints. Her hands slid around him to caress his tush, pushing the jeans further down until they hung on his hips.

Sam breathed hard, obviously trying to maintain his control. He was still leaning straight-armed against the door, when Naomi slipped to her knees. Her breath whispered across his throbbing hardness before she let her tongue lick at him. She looked up and smiled at the stunned, expectant look on Sam's face. Her yellow curls caught in the crisp black hairs of his thighs. She flipped her hair back with an impatient toss of her head, her hands holding him fast as her mouth encircled his engorged flesh. When Naomi snaked her tongue out to draw him further into her mouth, he moaned her name and closed his eyes.

Naomi had been on her knees for a man before, but never like this. The blood-sucking lawyer loved nothing better than to cajole, and, sometimes, to force her into this act; a death grip on her head or throat, thrusting into her, heedless of her gagging or choking. Demanding, criticizing, then leaving her used, but unfulfilled. It had taken an enormous leap of faith for her to offer herself this way to Sam. But she had wanted to, she wanted to bring him the selfless ecstasy he had given her on the piano in Chicago, and she had been working up her nerve since then.

This was not the same as with David. Sam was almost in a submissive stance. His hands were not on her except to occasionally stroke her hair. There were no demands from him, only murmured encouragements and compliments—*Sweet, sweet. Oh, darlin', that feels so good.* And he let her set the pace, drawing as much of him as she wanted into her mouth. He was getting harder as she sucked on him, swirling her tongue around the velvet tip of his penis, licking him, nibbling on him. *A big girl's erotic lollipop!*

He moaned now. No, *she* was moaning, *she* was straining to take more of him. *She* wanted him, *she* wanted to taste him, to make him lose control.

She transformed from supplicant to aggressor, her sounds of satisfaction competing with his deep groans.

"Enough!" Sam's voice startled her back to reality. He pulled her away from his throbbing flesh and up into his arms. She tried to tug free and reach for him.

Rubbing his thumb across her swollen lips, Sam whispered, "Darlin', darlin', I'm not as young as I used to be, and I don't want to waste this splendid erection you gave me by coming alone. I want to be inside you, I want to feel you coming when I let go." He was brushing kisses across her forehead, her eyes, cheeks, nose, everywhere he could reach.

Naomi was writhing against him. "I want you now, Sam, right now." Sam yanked her nightshirt up and leaned into the soft welcome of her breasts. The crisp hairs on his chest tortured her already hard nipples. Naomi tried to pull him closer by grasping his hips. His hard, hot flesh thrust against her stomach, still wet and throbbing from her mouth.

"We're not going to make it to the bed, Naomi. Wrap your arms around my neck. That's right, darlin'," he said as she complied. "Now, those long legs around my waist. Good girl." His large hands cupped her bottom, opening her to him. Then he was inside her. The force of his thrust bumped her head against the door, but she just held onto him more fiercely. He withdrew slightly, then, groaning, slid into her all the way. He stopped, breathing hard. He stood holding her like that, almost motionless, his forehead resting on hers.

"I can't wait, baby. I can't wait." Sam jerked his hips.

At the heated urgency of his words, Naomi felt her own release begin. She locked her legs around him and pulled his mouth to hers. The tremors were already rippling through her, clenching around him as he exploded into her. Spent, he held onto her as she followed him into ecstasy.

Later, it seemed *much* later, they slid to the floor in an exhausted heap. Sam started laughing, at the sight of his jeans tangled around his knees and Naomi's nightshirt twisted around her lush breasts, Winnie the Pooh all but hidden in the bunched up folds, and her sweatshirt hung crazily off one shoulder. Her moccasins were under him, though he didn't seem to have the strength to reach for them.

"Darlin', do you think we're ever going to make love properly in a real bed? I'm getting a little old for these romantic gymnastics we engage in. Not that I haven't enjoyed them, but my knees are starting to kill me and your butt must be sore."

"*Your* knees? Seems like I was on my knees tonight, Cowboy." Naomi laughed as she blew a strand of hair out of her eyes, unable to lift a hand to brush it away. "Or have you forgotten already?"

"Darlin', I will never forget the sight of all that shining sunlight hair of yours spread across my legs. And your hands on me. And your mouth. Dear Jesus God, Naomi, when you aren't taking the skin off my hide with that tongue of yours, you surely know how to use that sexy mouth. I just lose control with you."

"My assistant, Janice, calls that *instant Alzheimer's*. Says it works every time on her husband. Funny, I never seemed to get the hang of it before."

"Naomi, honey, you are one quick learner." Sam chuckled. "But, you have to know, the best thing about what you just did isn't how it made me feel, it's how it made you feel." Sam's hand rested on Naomi's knee, his thumb tracing lazy circles on her skin.

"There was a point where it went from being about me and went to being about you and your sensuality. If two people want each other and care about each other, they don't just want to get pleasure, they want to give pleasure. Seeing someone unravel at the touch of your hand, your mouth...that's one powerful aphrodisiac."

Naomi had stopped listening when Sam said *two people care about each other*. He cared about her, she hadn't chased him away with her questions, he wanted her *and* liked her. She wasn't sure how to feel about that. She liked Sam and God knew she wanted him, *all the time*. But, it had been years since she gave her heart away and watched the blood-sucking lawyer throw it down and grind it under his heel as he walked out on her. She'd patched it up and promised herself never to be that vulnerable again. And yet here she was, half naked on the floor of a hotel room with an aging country singer and her insides starting to melt all over again as his hand stroked up her thigh. *I'll think about it later,* she thought as she opened her legs to Sam's touch.

CHAPTER NINE

"Get me out of here. NOW!"

"I hate you. I want to go to Dad's. You're just jealous!"

"I want to live with Dad, at least he loves me."

"You're a terrible mother."

From Bozeman to Cheyenne to Denver, on and on went Jonah's e-mails. Every time Naomi opened her laptop, she was hit with another dose of adolescent outrage. *What happened to traditional letters from camp? Send me chewing gum and candy bars. At least I wouldn't have to read this garbage every day. What am I going to do? What am I going to do?*

Sitting in Sam's suite in Denver, just as the sun came up, Naomi dropped her head into her hands. She rubbed her aching forehead as she scrolled through Jonah's outpourings of spite.

All she ever wanted was for her son to be happy. And healthy. And a doctor. Well, at least some satisfying, well-paying career. Definitely not a lawyer! Everything she had done, including leaving his lying, cheating father, had been to ensure Jonah wanted for nothing, especially love and security. She struggled and sacrificed and sometimes, like now, she thought, it had been for nothing.

Naomi pounded her fist against her thigh, giving herself up to a momentary spurt of self-pity. *It is so fucking hard being the mom when the dad is a self-centered, egotistical asshole, caught up in the fantasy world of younger trophy wife and kewpie doll new baby.* To David, Jonah was a costly reminder of Naomi, and to his new wife an unwelcome remnant of his *other* marriage. Naomi still believed David loved their son, but it was obvious wife number two did not. Courtney constantly put David in a position of having to choose between his two children. Because David was under the spell of his new, much younger wife, he almost always chose his baby daughter.

I hope he suffers the guilt of the damned for eternity in Gehenom! Naomi hoped David felt some remorse for his failings as a father. She was sure he did—just not enough to do anything positive about it.

More often in the past year, David took out his frustration with the situation on Jonah. As a result, Jonah received from his father cancelled visits, unfulfilled promises, and weak excuses. Naomi tried to make it up to Jonah and tried not to speak against David, lest Jonah feel compelled to take sides. As a result, she became Jonah's emotional punching bag. *I take as much shit from that boy as I took from my father. And I swore I would never do that again. It got me nowhere with Pop, and it's getting me nowhere with Jonah.*

Naomi could hear Sam's muffled snores through the open door to the bedroom. She got up to stare out the window, as if the scene before her could provide answers to her dilemma about Jonah. Added to her mom guilt now was Naomi's growing self-reproach over her affair with Sam. She was having a good time on the tour; no, she was having a *great* time, and Jonah was so unhappy. *What kind of mother am I?*

Jewish guilt will get you every time! Our kids think their Jewish moms lay the guilt trip on them! They have no idea the guilt WE feel every time we have to say no. As was the case with most single moms, Naomi was responsible for dragging Jonah to the orthodontist, to Bar Mitzvah lessons, to the pediatrician, to the math tutor, and rarely to the *fun stuff.* That pleasure fell to his once-a-month-dad who, when he made himself available, took Jonah to the Yankees, the Giants, and the Knicks. Loud games, lots of junk food, plenty of souvenirs equaled Super Dad to Jonah. It also got David off the hook of having to have any real conversations with his son. *Dazzle 'em David*, they called him at the firm, lots of flash, not a lot of substance. But the clients and his son loved him. The clients didn't like the associates who gave them the bad news about their cases or accounts; none of that shit stuck to David, just like no shit stuck to him where Jonah was concerned. Naomi was the villain.

Well, that's a nice little pity party you're having there, sweetheart. Naomi turned away from the window and closed the laptop. She had called David twice and e-mailed him a dozen times to confirm he was going to Parents' Weekend at the camp that weekend. It was the least he could do after prevaricating on his invitation to the Hamptons. Jonah said he wanted her at camp, but she had attended all the other Parents' Weekends. *What the boy was really praying for was that his dad would come.*

In her last phone call just the day before, Naomi tried to explain the situation to Jonah.

"Son, you know your geography. I am in the middle of the Wild West. It's not like New York, where there is a flight any time of day to anywhere you want to go."

"I don't care where you are, Mom. You're supposed to be here. I'll probably be the only kid with no family here. But, you don't care."

"Jonah, you know I care and you know I love you, and I would be there if I could. Your dad has promised he will come for the weekend. I've reminded him four times about the date and time. I'm sure he will be there, and you will have a great time."

"Yeah, thanks, Mom. You probably pissed him off again, and he'll stay away just because you nagged him too much. Thanks a lot for nothing."

"He wouldn't do that, Jonah. And I'm sorry, you know I would be there if I could get there and get back to the tour in time."

He'd hung up on her again. Naomi was angry with Jonah and David. And herself. What she told Jonah was true, but it wasn't the real reason for her reluctance to return to New York. Sam was the reason.

She turned away from the laptop, and the anger and guilt it held, and walked back into the bedroom. At least there, at least for now, was comfort and warmth.

CHAPTER TEN

The night sky outside the bus was like black velvet, and the stars seemed like tiny white Christmas lights to him, twinkling and blinking in random designs. Sam felt a peace envelop him, the same peace he always felt when he returned to the deserts and mountains of the West. Shadows from distant peaks and plateaus danced across the highway, black on black. No other traffic was on the road before him; the tractor-trailers were a good hour ahead of him, he knew. He hummed the melody that stayed with him over the past several days, the one he heard outside Naomi's synagogue in Chicago. It was mixing in his brain with a new melody and a bit of a hymn he sang as a boy. *I've got to do something with this. The words won't come, though. I should play it for Tyrone.*

The heavy curtains behind the driver's seat parted, and there was Naomi. Her cheeks were flushed with sleep, and her eyes still had a heavy, slumberous look. All that blonde mane was caught up on top of her head and tumbled around her face and neck in wild disarray. She yawned and stretched, her softly curved belly showing above the top of her cutoffs. She had thrown one of his denim shirts on after the heat of the day had disappeared with the sun. Sam's throat was suddenly dry, and he could feel the fit of his jeans altering as he stared at Naomi in the rear-view mirror.

Watching her, words played through his mind—something he remembered from college, Lord Byron, maybe. He couldn't get it out of his mind:

She walks in beauty, like the night,
Of cloudless climes and starry skies;
And all that's best of dark and bright,
Meet in her aspect and her eyes....

Maybe he could put those words to the melody in his head.

"Well, hello, Cowboy. Where's Charlie?" Naomi asked as she rolled her head on that long slender neck made for kissing and biting.

"He had a headache from the sun today. I sent him back to take some aspirin and sleep it off in my bed."

"Damn. I just had a very graphic dream about you and that bed. Made me horny." She laughed, somewhat uncertainly. Her forays into sexual overtures with him were still few and far between and hesitant. Sam cursed to himself. *Damn that asshole she had been married to—he made her so uncertain of her sexuality and her appeal.*

"Well, I'm driving until we reach Santa Fe." He smiled at her ruefully.

"Perhaps we could just pull over, for a few minutes..." Naomi's voice was a quiet plea.

"Can't do that, darlin'. Everybody would wake up for sure, so unless you want an audience, there wouldn't be anything we could do." His blue eyes watched her closely in the mirror and he saw her hands start wringing the loose ends of the denim shirt. Then those perfect white teeth started chewing on her lush lower lip. *She wants me.* Sam thought maybe now was the time to undo some of the damage her husband had done to her.

"Maybe we can work something out up here, darlin'. Are you already wet for me?" He said it softly. Her eyes widened, surprised as realization dawned.

"What do you mean? I thought we could sneak on back to your room, but if Charlie is there, and we can't stop the bus…."

"Well, just because my hands are occupied with driving doesn't mean we can't use your hands. You just do what I tell you, and we'll have you feeling much better in no time." Sam flashed a seductive smile at her. And his words made her blush. Naomi stood there staring at him. Sam frowned with worry. *Oh, God, have I pushed her too far? I just want to free that wonderful spirit of hers and let her see how much power she has.*

⟨⟩

"You want my hands on you while you're driving? That can't be wise, and I don't know how that's going to help me, Sam." Her voice was shaky.

"It's not going to help me, darlin', it's going to help you. I'll be suffering the tortures of the damned watching you get off while I have to keep my hands on the wheel."

"You want me to…you want me to…touch myself so you can watch?" she almost squeaked. Naomi was shocked and titillated at the same time. She could feel the familiar tightening in her abdomen and the traitorous wetness between her legs. She licked her lips and Sam groaned.

"Just 'til we can make love, Naomi. You need to come; you're starting to shake with the need of it. I can see your nipples even through that heavy shirt. C'mon, do it for me, and you can have *this* as soon as we get to the hotel. You can have it all night long. I'll make you come a dozen times." His hand cupped the visible bulge in his jeans.

"I can wait," she said, her voice hitching as she watched his hardness swell even more, straining at the restriction of the soft denim.

"Well, what if I was to say you don't get this unless you let me watch you come right here and right now."

"I'd say it will be a frosty day in hell when I take orders from you or submit to your threats. Been there, done that, thank you." She was getting angry and she was hurt by what she thought was his attempt to bully her for his own gratification.

"No, darlin', you've never been there. You followed your husband's orders in bed, and you never got a minute's satisfaction, did you? You still think the man has all the power in sex. You still think you have to do what the man wants to get any pleasure in bed. That's what happens when you go to bed with adolescents who look like men. A real man knows to pleasure his woman first if he really wants to have great sex. If he's not willing to do that, he might as well beat off by himself!" His voice was a harsh whip as he berated Naomi's ex.

"What do you suggest I do first?" she asked, stiffly.

"That's more like it, darlin'. Haven't you ever teased a man? Don't you know what just looking at you does to me?" He grinned at her.

He thinks this is some kind of game? Well, she was going to take his dare and he was going to pay for it. She smiled back at him and tried to relax.

"Just unbutton the rest of that shirt, and let me see what excuse for underwear you've got on tonight. Go ahead, honey, there's nobody going to see you." Naomi could see no lights ahead of them on the road and there were no sounds from the back of the bus—except Tyrone's snoring.

Naomi's hands trembled but she pulled the three snaps apart. The too-large shirt still hung virtually closed across her chest.

"Now, darlin', just slip that shirt back so I can see those big beautiful breasts of yours." Naomi's head was down as she pulled the front of the shirt apart, revealing full breasts caught in a net of dark blue lace. She looked up and saw Sam's eyes in the rearview mirror, watching her.

"Honey, there ought to be a law against the under things you wear. I can see your nipples right through that lace. Are they hard for me yet? I love to suck on them until they get hard. Your nipples are like the blackberries we picked back home when I was a kid. Ripe and luscious and I could never get enough of them." She felt her nipples harden and stretch the lace of her bra at his words. She gasped at her swift reaction to his voice.

She liked it when he whispered dirty little things in her ear while they were making love, but standing apart from him and listening was not the same. Naomi wasn't sure she liked it, but her stomach was twisting at the sound of his soft, provocative words, and she was finding it hard to breathe.

"Put your hands on your nipples, Naomi, and tell me how hard they are." Almost of their own volition, her hands slid up to cup her breasts. Her thumbs brushed across her nipples, causing them to peak even more.

"They're hard," she whispered, not daring to look at him. She took a deep breath and said, huskily, "They're as hard as your cock."

He jerked in reaction to that last. She had never said that particular word to him, and the object of her remark swelled visibly in response.

"I can't see them, darlin'. Just unsnap that little piece of midnight that's covering them up. Please. I just want to look at you." His gaze was hot, reflected in the rear-view mirror.

Naomi swallowed hard and undid the clasp on the front of her bra. She pushed the cups away from her breasts, allowing them to swing free. Still standing slightly behind him, she looked into the reflection of his eyes in the mirror. They were burning, no longer that cold flat blue of the first time they had met, but the blue fire found at the hot center of a flame. He sucked in his breath as her hands caressed the satin white skin of her breasts and belly. She was breathing hard now, too.

"Come a little closer to me, honey," Sam coaxed her. She stepped toward him and felt his free hand slide up the back of her thigh and into the baggy leg of her cut-offs. His fingers probed farther until they were between her legs, brushing against the moist lace. "You get so wet, darlin'. I'll bet I could slide three fingers inside you right now and you could take all of me."

Naomi swayed closer to him. She held on to the chrome pole behind the driver's seat with one hand, the other hand unconsciously stroking her belly.

Sam pulled his hand away from Naomi's crotch, then reached down and unsnapped his own jeans. The zipper went next, and then he was free, hard and erect, pulsing with his own growing desire. Naomi's eyes widened as she stared at Sam's lap. She chewed on her lower lip in frustration. And anticipation. Sam groaned. Then he nodded toward her.

"Well, darlin', why don't you just loosen those shorts until you can reach inside."

It was as if she were someone else. Sam's sexy words and outrageously erotic suggestions were like little whips of fire along her nerves. She was starting to shake with her desire for him, for release. She didn't know what his game was, and she didn't want to play but she was compelled to do so. Naomi never had a chance to let her desires run free. The blood-sucking lawyer had been a selfish, unimaginative lover, and after him, she had been too self-conscious of her age—and the changes in her body—to believe she was attractive to men. After all, she had reasoned, if she couldn't satisfy a man when she was in her twenties, with firm breasts and a flat belly, what hope did she have in her thirties, with full, soft breasts, a curving tummy and all the other changes child-bearing and maturity had wreaked on her body.

"Sam." It was more a moan than a plea. But her fingers were already working at the button of her cut-offs. She paused. But she was too far gone now. She let her fingers disappear into her shorts.

"Are you wet for me, honey? Just slide your finger inside and tell me what you feel." His hard flesh was throbbing as Naomi did as he requested. He watched her hesitant movements through narrowed eyes. Suddenly, Sam grabbed her hand and pulled it free of her panties. Her shorts dropped to floor, loosened by his quick movement. Pulling her hand to his mouth, he sucked on her fingers, tasting her passion.

The air was thick with desire, surrounding her, heating her skin until she felt like she was on fire. With the gentle tugging on her fingers, Naomi could feel the tension coiling in her abdomen and knew she was close to losing control. She stepped out of her shorts and in one motion, swung her leg over Sam and planted herself firmly in his lap.

"What the hell…?" Sam sputtered as he reached around her to grasp the steering wheel with both hands. Naomi's arms were around Sam's neck as she tried to get closer to his heat. Her mouth was a wet brand on his neck, and her legs held his hips in a vise-like grip. She was so tight against him, she knew he could feel the tremors from the apex of her thighs, and her nipples were like points of fire against the thin T-shirt covering his chest.

All she knew was she had to have him inside her and soon. His game had brought her close to orgasm, but she held back, her memories kept her from going over the edge. All those memories of all those long, lonely nights after her divorce—and even some before it—when she writhed in her need to be held, to be kissed, to be made love to—and the only release came from her own hand. Not again, at least not as long as Sam was there. She knew what she needed, and it wasn't an empty, solo orgasm. It was the joining she experienced with Sam, uniting within her body, two becoming one, yet both of them soaring free as passion erupted and sent them flying. And falling back to Earth, knowing he was there to catch her.

Naomi lifted herself, with her arms still wrapped around Sam, and felt the tip of his rock-hard erection pressing against the thin, wet lace straining across the opening between her legs. She reached between them and pushed her thong out of the way. Then he was inside her. Naomi rocked her hips as she settled in his lap again, his hardness filling her, sliding home, all the way, until his coarse black curls and her soft blonde ones meshed.

"God, Naomi, what are you doing to me? I am close to exploding here. Jesus, you are so hot and wet, like creamy silk." He groaned. "Whatever you want, you're gonna have to take, darlin'. I have to keep my hands on the wheel and my eyes on the road. And I can't move. Baby, this is all about you. What do you want? What do you need?"

Then Naomi whispered in his ear, "I'm coming, Sam, come with me. Come with me, baby, please. I need to feel you, I need YOU!"

The spasms were starting to take her, she was whimpering in his ear, against his neck and then her mouth was on his, moaning. Grabbing a hand full of hair, Sam pulled her head to the side so he could still see the road. Groaning into her neck, all he said was "Yes!" And then he spewed hot bursts of life into her, filling her, as she clenched around him, holding him tight inside.

When it was over, Naomi slumped against Sam, her mouth soft and wet against his shoulder, her hands pressed against his chest. His hand tangled in her hair, holding her head against him. They both dripped with sweat, even in the air-conditioned coolness of the bus.

"Darlin', are you okay?" Sam's voice finally rasped, softly, in her ear. She couldn't answer. She was completely spent, the aftershocks of their orgasms still running through her, inner muscles clenching around his still-hard flesh.

"I'm not moving, I'm never moving. I'm staying here until we get to Phoenix or wherever the hell it is we're going."

He chuckled. "Have I told you lately how much I love those cut-offs? They come off you as fast as green corn through the hired girl."

"That makes no sense, Sam."

"Well, excuse me, honey, but I'm not thinking too straight right now. I think my eyes might be permanently crossed." He laughed. "It's an old expression of my granddad's; I haven't thought of it in years."

Naomi lifted her head and looked at him. He looked as stunned as she felt. "What the hell was that all about, Sam? Do you play that game often? A way to break the monotony of an all-night drive?"

"Darlin', I have *never* done *that* before, cross my heart." He glanced at her. "I guess we both learned a little lesson tonight, honey. You may not be real experienced, but you sure are game. And I have a lot less control than I thought I did, at least with you. You got to me tonight. I don't know how I feel about that," he ended somberly.

Naomi got real quiet. She felt it too, an elemental joining, that moment when you see inside someone's soul and realize that he has as many wounds as you do.

Taking a deep breath, Naomi spoke, pushing the words out in a rush.

"The…um…my husband used to criticize my body. My breasts were too big, my *tush* too wide, even when we were dating. He said it as a joke but I knew he meant it. He told me I was lucky he loved me, even with the way I looked. I believed him, I never had many boyfriends in high school and then I met him my first year of college. After we were married and I got pregnant, he constantly picked at me. Your body is a mess when you're pregnant, Sam. My breasts got bigger—too big—he said I looked like a cow, and that's how I felt. And the stretch marks! Then after, I nursed Jonah, and David had more comments to make. Then, finally, he just said I was disgusting. My belly never got flat again, and I must have done a million sit-ups. My breasts were soft, and some of the stretch marks never went away. I know men want to have women with perfect bodies, and mine just never was."

"Your husband is a spoiled little boy who ought to be horsewhipped." Sam spat. "Look at me. Look at me, Naomi." He nudged her head up with his shoulder until he could see her eyes.

"You've seen me, well, pretty much all of me. I have scars all over, from football, rodeo, fights. You don't flinch when you see them. You don't seem to find me…unattractive. I got my scars from foolishness. You have marks on your body from giving life, from giving that asshole a son. And he has the nerve to criticize you, to make you feel like less of a woman. He better hope I never get my hands on him, or a few marks will be the least of his worries!" Sam's voice was at once both harsh and tender. His lips brushed her hair before he continued.

"You don't have scars, honey, you have badges of honor. I love that mark on your hip, looks like a silver crescent moon and when I get you in a bed, I'm going to kiss it and every other mark on this warm sexy body. Don't ever feel ashamed, Naomi, at least not around me." He paused and grinned at her, lightening the mood of the moment. "I love your body, even now, when I think my thighs have gone to sleep. C'mon, darlin', and see if you can lift that sweet *tush* off me and get some clothes on before anyone wakes up."

Naomi kissed him and, groaning, slipped from his lap. Pulling on her shorts and snapping up the front of the denim shirt, she found she had tears in her eyes from his anger on her behalf and his soothing words. *God help me, but I think I'm falling in love with him.* She stepped behind him, bending to put her arms around his neck, feeling like she had the whole world in her hands. He finished adjusting his jeans and clasped her two hands in one of his. Lost in their thoughts, they stayed like that as the miles flew by into the night behind them.

CHAPTER ELEVEN

"Ms. Stein? This is Trudy Hammer at Sunrise Lake Camp. We have a bit of an emergency here with Jonah. He insisted we call his father yesterday, but we have been unable to reach Mr. Bregman and action needs to be taken now." The voice was scratchy in Naomi's ear, but the meaning was clear. *Trouble*.

Twenty minutes later, Naomi was throwing clothes into her suitcase while barking orders to Janice on her cell phone. It was Monday morning in Santa Fe, and Jonah had run away during the campfire on Parents' Weekend—a weekend he was suffering through alone because David failed to show up. He couldn't get out of a party for very important clients on Fire Island, or so he told Jonah during a phone call on Saturday morning, just an hour before he was supposed to be driving through the birch bark columns holding the *Welcome Parents!* sign at the entrance to Sunrise Lake Camp. Jonah waited by the sign, hoping David would change his mind, until mid-afternoon. The counselors dragged him along with some of the foreign campers until the campfire.

He was missing when they did bed check just before midnight. They found him on the highway into town, trying to hitch a ride to the Greyhound bus station. Jonah was fine, Mrs. Hammer had assured Naomi, but he had to be sent home. The camp had a strict policy on runaways. Immediate suspension.

Naomi had tried to reach David on his cell and his home phone; finally, in desperation, she had called his office. His secretary informed her he was *in court* and could not be interrupted. Naomi hung up without leaving a message. She wouldn't trust David to see to Jonah anyway. So, she had begged her sister, Miriam, to take him for the next week, until she located David and made arrangements. Her sister grudgingly agreed, but Naomi knew she would hold it over her head for years and would make sure her mother heard all about how Miriam had come to the rescue. As she listened to Janice recite the flight arrangements, Naomi's mind screamed like a banshee.

I will have to pay for this forever. I will need to lavish Miriam with gifts when I drop Jonah off AND when I pick him up. I am going to ground him until he is thirty-five. I am going to lock him in his room with no phone, no computer, no television, and no food. But, I am going to kill his father. This is justifiable homicide; no jury in the world will convict me. Maybe I will just plead insanity because these two MALES are making me crazy.

Naomi answered the insistent knocking on the door to her room, grim-faced, nodding silently to the telephone glued to her ear. She turned and walked away from Sam, back to the clothes strewn across her unmade bed, the unmade bed he'd left only a few hours before. She blushed at the memory of a naked Sam, sprawled on his stomach, laughing and gasping she was going to kill him—but he would die with a smile on his face—after a particularly energetic bout of lovemaking.

Naomi slammed her cell phone on the nightstand and started shoving more clothes into her bag. At Sam's grunted expletive—*fuck*—she looked up, focusing on him for the first time. His face was a mask of anger and shock.

"Were you going to tell me you were leaving or just let me find out when you didn't get on the bus tonight?" His hands clenched at his sides, and his eyes flashed with cold fury.

"Sam, I was going to tell you as soon as the arrangements were made." He turned his back on her and strode to the window. She came up behind him and gently forced him to turn and look at her.

"Sam. It's Jonah. He's been kicked out of camp. I can't find David so I have to go back to New York to get him."

"Naomi, Jesus, I'm sorry. What happened?" Sam's voice was full of tender concern.

She explained to him what had happened as she walked back and forth between the bed and the bathroom, her hands full of lingerie and cosmetics. She had just dropped shampoo and hair brushes into her overflowing luggage when Sam started laughing.

"Darlin', what are you worried about? Go fetch him and bring him back here. I never met a kid who didn't love goin' on the bus with the boys."

"Are you crazy. Sam? What would he do all day? He can't be running around with the roadies...can he?" The idea was appealing. Maybe it would work. Miriam was being difficult, as always, and David would remain *incommunicado* until the shit storm he had caused died down.

"Sure he can, and he can hang with me and the band too. Some of the guys have brought their kids during school breaks, and my niece and nephew used to tour with us every summer when they were younger. Now Bobbi considers tours *her* summer vacation and makes them stay on the farm with their dad."

"Well, I have to go get him today, in any event. The camp won't let him stay." She still sounded doubtful.

"Naomi, remember we have a short hiatus starting tomorrow. The guys have to drive the trucks to Philadelphia for the show next week. The band will be flying East and meet them there. I have to do a few radio promos for the New York City show this fall. You can meet up with us in Philadelphia on Friday. You won't miss anything."

In a few sentences, Sam had it all worked out for her. One phone call to Tommy, and the plan was set in motion. As Naomi flew back to New York that afternoon, she considered how neatly Sam had stepped in and solved her problem like it was nothing. When she first met him, she thought him cold and distant and a bit arrogant. But, now that they had spent time together, she realized it was just a façade he put up to strangers he didn't trust, like reporters and promoters. Never with his band or with the fans. With his friends, he had such an easy manner. No matter what cropped up, he seemed to meet it with equanimity and an innate good humor. *Where had that balance come from*? Naomi made a note to herself to discover the source of Sam's peaceful nature. She had never been able to find that level of inner peace. Must have something to do with having kids, she thought.

Naomi sipped at her glass of wine as her mind drifted back over the last weeks with Sam. They spent so much time together. But still, there were depths to Sam she only saw in those rare moments after lovemaking when his inner guard slipped a bit. A natural reserve? Or, a secret inner boundary no one was allowed to cross?

Would he let her in? She was not certain whether it was the reporter or the woman who was posing that question. Either way, she wanted answers. Her relationship with Sam was unexpected and often uncomfortable. And inexplicable. But she wanted it and him.

"And, what in hell am I going to tell Jonah?" she muttered to herself as she stared off into the clouds.

CHAPTER TWELVE

Explaining Sam to Jonah was the least of Naomi's concerns. Jonah Bregman was definitely not happy. He had been a bit abashed at the camp, sitting amidst his trunk and camp bags, waiting for his mother, obviously wishing for his dad. He knew he was in deep trouble, but he apparently figured at least he was out of camp and his mom would take him with her to the Cape. It seemed, to her troubled son, anything was better than hanging out with a bunch of stupid kids.

Now he made his feelings very well known. He whined about being stuck on a plane to Philadelphia, and no phone call from his dad. He bristled when Naomi informed him the Cape was not going to happen. She was still so *pissed*!

"Mom," he began. Naomi turned to him, glaring over the top of her black sunglasses. He should know *that* look. Jonah fell back into silence. Then the words tumbled out.

"It isn't my fault that the kids at camp are jerks. It isn't my fault my dad didn't show up for Parents' Weekend. Dad said it was your fault because you always make everything so difficult and unpleasant. You make it hard for him to come around and you're always demanding more money. And not for me."

"Jonah, you know that isn't true. You see me deposit every one of your dad's checks at your bank, not at my bank. You see the checks I write for your regular school and Hebrew School and the orthodontist and everything else. Those checks come out of my account, not yours. I've even shown you your savings account book, you can check every entry. The only withdrawals are when you want to buy something for Bubbe or me with your own money."

Jonah just turned away from her, to stare glumly out the window, shutting her out of his world.

Naomi sighed and let her thoughts drift away from the troubled boy beside her. Jonah was so unhappy, so angry, so remote. She had tried to reach through all that at camp, but he froze her out, wanting only his father. She knew that feeling. Naomi had wanted her father, too. He had been so disappointed she wasn't a boy. From an early age, she knew his disappointment but thought if she excelled, if she showed an interest in his interests, he would thaw. But, he was so conservative he viewed her attempts to please him as a lack of femininity on her part, as her failure to *know her place*. So she was doubly damned in his eyes: not the hoped-for male heir and not a proper girl like Miriam.

Her mother witnessed this sad situation and tried to smooth Naomi's way in the family, without incurring the wrath of her husband. But Naomi also knew her mother was completely devoted to her father. They survived Hell together, and no one was more important to her mother than Alex Stein. Since Auschwitz, they had only had each other, with no family or close friends left for either of them. Naomi's mother had been a buffer between Naomi and her father, and Miriam had slipped easily into the void. It seemed no one had ever been there for Naomi; there were times Naomi resented the hell out of both her mother and her sister. *I guess that's how Jonah feels about me. I try to make it easy with his dad, and all I seem to do is alienate him.*

Silently shaking her head, Naomi finally realized she couldn't make David want Jonah, and she couldn't make Jonah stop wanting David—just as her mother had not been able to make her husband love Naomi or to help ease Naomi's need for her father. The headache that plagued her all day seemed to ease a bit. It was long past the time to just play it straight with Jonah, no more excuses for his father. And no more easy ride for Jonah, either. It was going to be the truth now between them; she was tired of being the mediator. Her statements about their finances had been a small beginning. She would just have to keep on that path with him.

First we have to deal with Philadelphia. And Sam. I sure hope some of that brotherly love will rub off on Jonah and me.

CHAPTER THIRTEEN

Sweating, Sam knocked softly on the door to the suite he had booked for Naomi and her son. It was early, just a little after six, but already Philadelphia was sweltering. *Philadelphia in July... How did those guys manage this heat and writing the Declaration of Independence? And without air-conditioning.* He didn't hear a sound from the sitting room on the other side of the door. They were probably still asleep. Sam used his key to silently open the door. Stepping quickly inside, he wiped his brow as he looked around the spacious rooms that were the mirror image of his own suite across the hall. Naomi had arrived late last night, and Sam was anxious to see her. Only two days apart and he had missed her more than he had missed anyone in years.

Through the open door of the bedroom to his left, Sam spotted a backpack, sneakers, and a Yankees cap tossed on the floor. Assuming it must be the kid's room, he veered to the right, across the sitting area, to the larger bedroom. He quietly pushed the door open. His gaze immediately found Naomi.

There she was, sprawled across the big bed, arms and legs akimbo, tangled in the sheets. The arresting beauty of her face in repose struck him again. Not a classic beauty, by any means, but a pleasing combination of features that resonated deep within him. All that golden mane of hers spread on the pillow and her shoulder, the bit of sunlight peeking through a crack in the heavy drapes, playing across the curls, turning them to yellow fire. Her ridiculous Pooh nightshirt hiked up over a rounded hip on one side and dipped low on her shoulder, revealing the curve of a lush breast.

Sam quietly closed the door behind him, locking it. He felt a bone-deep need to touch Naomi. Kicking off his running shoes, he

walked silently over the deep carpet to her. She was making that
funny little guppy noise she did when she was fast asleep. Sam
grinned as he sat down beside her on the bed, his hand already
caressing the cool flesh of her hip. He ran his hand down her thigh,
then back up, past her hip, pushing the nightshirt up even higher.
Winnie the Pooh's funny face scrunched out of view as Sam swept
his hand across her tummy. Naomi moaned softly and turned
toward his touch, almost instinctively arching and stretching into
his caress.

Her moan went straight to Sam's gut, tightening him, hardening
him, surprising the hell out of him. His hands shook as he pulled
his own sweaty shirt over his head. Without thinking, he pushed
the nightshirt farther up, up to her breasts and over. Her nipples
hardened to sharp points in the cool air; Sam couldn't resist a quick
nibble. Naomi moaned again, deep and soft, still slumbering but
moving into him. Her legs shifted, opening her to him. He touched
her there, just at the apex of her thighs, his fingers brushing those
tight golden curls. He felt her warm wetness, her arousal evident
even as she slumbered on, her body responding to his touch of its
own volition.

He throbbed hard against his running shorts, the need pulsing
through him, centering there. He pushed her legs farther apart,
stroking her thighs, his hands coming to rest on her belly. His
thumb pushed into the curls, into her heat, until he found the hard
nub of her clit. Stroking softly, he felt her start to quiver. *God. I
have to have her. Now.*

Whispering her name, Sam drew off his shorts and knelt
between her legs. His hands swept up and down their smooth
length as he pulled her to him, pulled her up onto his thighs.
Gripping her hips, he eased into her, slowly, gently, calling her to
him.

Naomi's eyes fluttered open. She had been having the hottest
dream about Sam, so hot she could almost feel him inside her. She
blinked. And then her eyes opened wide. He *was* inside her,
gliding in and out, watching her, with eyes so blue, so intent.

"Sam, Sam," she moaned, her tongue licking across her dry lips,
waking to him. Her passion climbed as she started to meet his
thrusts, reaching out to cover his hands with her own. He pulled

her tight onto his cock and held her as he fucked her hard and fast. And then he came, jetting his fiery fluid into her, his head thrown back, almost grimacing with the intensity of his orgasm. He was done before she had really begun. Shocked, Naomi lay motionless as Sam eased out of her and flopped next to her on the bed.

"Damn," he laughed, "I just came in to see if you wanted breakfast and there you were, all sleepy and sexy. I couldn't resist, darlin', I just had to have you." He was still laughing when he reached for her.

"Don't touch me." Naomi snapped at him, pulling her nightshirt down over her still hard nipples. She squirmed away from him, trying to rise from the rumpled bed. "You've had your fuck, now I have to clean up." Yanking Winnie the Pooh over her belly and butt, Naomi shot out of bed and stalked to the bathroom.

"What the hell?" Sam sputtered. He followed her into the bathroom. She was already in the walk-in shower stall, steam rising above the glass doors.

The heat pulsed off her body as Naomi started scrubbing. Her eyes closed, the water coursed down her body, she shook with anger and frustration, as she scrubbed. *Just like David!* She had been half-waiting for this moment, for Sam to show his true colors. *Take, take, take.* Typical man! *Wham, bam, thank you ma'am.* Naomi beat herself up at the same time she cursed Sam and his entire gender. *Stupid, stupid, stupid!* Her hand whacked the slick tile, hard. *How could I have been so stupid...again!* She turned into the shower spray; let her head hang down under the pulsing wet heat, trying to wash his touch away.

Sam stepped into the steam. His hands reached out, gripped her arms as her head came up and she whipped around. "Let go of me! Get your hands off me! Now!" Naomi hurled the words at him through gritted teeth. Tempers flared.

"I am not letting go of you until you calm down and tell me what the fuck just happened in there!" The words hissed out of Sam's mouth. Naomi just glared at him.

"If you don't know, I am not going to tell you," she said with the exquisite logic of a deeply wronged female.

"If looks could kill, I would be dead and bleeding down that drain right now."

She turned her face away from him.

"Naomi," he whispered, trying to pull her to him.

Naomi wouldn't look at him and struggled to break his grip on her. Sam's hands tightened on her elbows, pulling her into his embrace. Arms wrapped around her, he held her tight as she fought him. *Damn, if my wiggling isn't arousing him all over again.*

His hardness pressed into her belly. Then she stopped suddenly and slumped. It was as if the fight just seeped right out of her.

"Sam, just let me go, please," she muttered into his chest.

"Look at me. Look at me, Naomi," Sam pleaded. She lifted her head from his chest, pushing her matted blonde hair away from her face. Her tear-filled eyes finally met his. He asked softly, "What is it, darlin'?"

"I'm tired, Sam, I am so damn tired. I'm tired of fighting you. Just leave me alone." Her voice was a sorrowful whisper that made him cringe.

"I'll leave you alone if you just tell me what's wrong."

"I can't. I can't talk about it." She sighed and tried to turn away. Sam wouldn't let her. He bent his head to kiss her, but she turned her face from him. His warm lips were on her cheek, her forehead, the tip of her nose, the corner of her mouth. She sighed again, a deep, raspy sound that tore at his heart.

"Tell me, tell me," he muttered as he rained kisses on her face, "I'll make it better."

Naomi knew Sam would not stop holding her and kissing her unless she let it out, so she told him. Told him David had done the same thing to her, the last time he was in her bed. Woke her from a dead sleep, already inside her. She hadn't been ready, and he hurt her. When she tried to pull away from him, he slapped her across the face. He had never hit her before. She had been momentarily stunned. Then she had pulled her leg up and kicked him hard in the chest. He fell off her, onto the bed, as she scrambled to pull the sheets up and get away from him. Sitting up, he laughed at her. Told her she had always been a lousy lay. She told him to go to hell. He laughed again and said he was going, but not to hell. He was going to Courtney's. He had only come home to get a few things and when he saw her asleep, he figured he would give Naomi a sympathy fuck since she was not likely to get laid again anytime soon. Then he walked out the door.

Naomi's voice had dropped to a whisper. Sam's hands had not

stopped stroking her arms through the telling. She could feel his eyes on her. She straightened her shoulders, sucked up her courage and finished her tale. "And he was right. There wasn't really anyone after that for a long time. Not 'til you."

"And then I come in after you've had a bitch of a day and night and wake you up pretty much the same way. Damn. Naomi, I am so sorry." She stared at him. His hands tightened on her arms. "But, I'm pissed off, too. Don't you know me well enough yet to know I wouldn't just fuck you and leave you unsatisfied? I just wanted to catch my breath, and then I was going to take care of you. But you were up and out of bed before I could do or say anything."

Then he kissed her. Hard. He kissed her with what seemed like all the anger he felt toward her bastard of a husband, all the sorrow for her damage, all the passion he had for her and all the need she had awakened in him to cherish and protect her. Knots of her wet tangled hair twined around his fingers as he held her, as though he couldn't get enough of her lips, her mouth, her tongue. Naomi whimpered then wrapped her arms around his neck, holding onto him as though she was drowning.

His lips left her mouth and traveled down her neck to her collarbone, and below. Naomi's grip loosened as Sam's mouth fastened on her nipple, suckling as though he was a starving infant, drawing the stiff peak into his mouth. Sam's hands roamed all over her, caressing, sweeping away her anger and her shame. Eyes closed, weak, she leaned back against the tile as he knelt before her, his lips everywhere, his mouth honing in on the throbbing bit of flesh at her core.

Sam pulled her to him, holding her tight against his mouth as he plundered her nether lips in the same way his tongue had been plundering her mouth. Devouring her, eating her, healing her. Sending her into passion alone, but not lonely, because he held onto her, caressing her, encouraging her to let go. Naomi came on a weak cry, falling into his arms as the spasms coursed through her, slipping down until she rested against him on the shower floor, the hot water feeling almost cool on her fevered skin.

He held her as she cried, tears and shower spray mingling on her flushed face. She cried for her ruined marriage, she cried for the father and then the husband who had rejected her because she was not, could not be, what they wanted. She cried for her son, left fatherless because of her. She cried for Sam, alone, damaged, hurt too, but still reaching out for her. She cried because she was falling in love with him and could not, did not want to, stop. Finally, she cried because she knew he would hold her and care for her more than anyone else ever had.

CHAPTER FOURTEEN

A couple of hours later, wrapped in one of the hotel's luxurious robes, Naomi sat before the wide window in the living area of the suite, devouring breakfast. The small, white linen covered table groaned under the weight of still-warm bagels, cream cheese, fluffy scrambled eggs, fresh fruit and a massive teapot. *It was good to be back on the East Coast for decent bagels.*

Relaxed but a little sore, she was sure she still blushed from what transpired just a few feet away, behind the closed door of her bedroom. And the bathroom. *I could not make this shit up if I wanted to.* She giggled and reached for the other half of the bagel she just finished.

"What's so funny?" The smile left Naomi's flushed face at the grumpy question from Jonah. He stood scowling in the doorway of his room, rumpled and cute in a Yankees T-shirt and white boxers, his hair standing on end from a restless night's sleep.

Her shoulders slumped under the extravagant softness of the robe, then straightened, as Naomi transformed from woman to mother, from blushing and amused, to flushed and frustrated with her errant son. *Why does it have to be like this?* She had been the sun, the moon, and the stars to Jonah from the day he was born. As an infant and a toddler, Jonah always reached for his mother. And she was always there. His father worked long hours and longer weeks. David only became the center of Jonah's world when he removed himself completely from it. *Why did our easy camaraderie disappear with David?*

Ignoring the rude question seemed the most reasonable tack to take, so Naomi motioned Jonah to join her at the small, heavily-laden table. "I ordered bagels and scrambled eggs and fruit and yogurt for us. There's a nice cold glass of chocolate milk for you, too." She pointed it out to him, when he came to stand beside her.

Jonah slouched in the chair opposite Naomi and gulped down the milk. It left a brown mustache on his upper lip, where it competed with the fine growth of hair that hadn't been there when he went to camp. *Or had it? What else have I missed? Where is my little boy?*

There was a short rap on the door to the suite, then it popped open to reveal William's smiling face. "Hey, you guys decent?" Jonah jumped up and ran to William, high-fiving him and boogying into his arms.

"Man, you got sprung from camp? How'd you pull that off?" Tucking Jonah under his arm, William didn't wait for an answer, zeroing in on the bagels and cream cheese, missing the strained silence between mother and son.

"I thought he might like to hang out with you and the guys for the last week before break, so I got him yesterday." Jonah gave Naomi a surprised glance, obviously thinking she had been about to rat him out to William. Naomi merely raised an eyebrow. She knew Jonah liked and respected William because the photographer treated Jonah like an equal and occasionally let him experiment with one of his cameras.

"Cool." William muttered between bites. "Sam said you wanted to bring Jonah on tour, let him be a roadie for a while. Nice of him to okay it, don't you think?" Naomi nodded. So Sam had given her the credit for this idea, had not let anyone know the turmoil she was in because of Jonah's bad behavior at camp, and had covered for her abrupt departure two days ago. *He took care of everyone.*

"Well, I know how much Jonah likes to hang with you, William, and I hoped he'd have the chance to see you before you went to Morocco. Besides, he hasn't been on the road with me before, and this seemed like a good tour to...."

"Yeah, babe, certainly not as rowdy as some of the ones we've been on. Remember the Rolling Stones the last time? Hard to believe that Keith is ever gonna get old!"

Naomi cleared her throat and shot William a look. Jonah was paying a bit too much attention to the details of this conversation. He did *not* need to hear anecdotes about those wild days.

"Okay, well, they asked me to come up and see if you all

wanted to go to a baseball game this afternoon. Tommy scored some tickets for the Orioles game, and we gotta get going if we're going to make it to Baltimore."

Naomi looked over at Jonah, trying to gauge the mood. She didn't want to reward him for his bad behavior at camp, but she didn't want a battle either. He watched her through narrowed eyes. "I guess I'm up for a game if Jonah is." Naomi was deliberately noncommittal. "But he isn't a big fan of the Orioles, you know."

William smiled and said, "Yeah, I know, it's just the Orioles. But, we got pretty good seats, and Camden Yards is still new." William paused. "And they're playing the Yankees."

Jonah whooped and did a little victory dance. "Mom, we gotta go, can we go, please?" He was her little boy again; excited about a trip to the ballpark, just like he used to be when they would *schlep* to the Bronx to watch the Yankees from the cheap seats in the bleachers.

"How much time do we have? Baltimore is, what, two hours away?" Naomi asked as she rose from the table and headed toward her bedroom.

"If you are downstairs in fifteen minutes, we should make it fine." William answered as he took her seat and reached for the fruit.

"Jonah, brush your teeth," Naomi called out as they both rushed to their bedrooms, leaving William to enjoy the remnants of breakfast.

Exactly fourteen minutes later, they were at the elevator, sporting Yankees T-shirts and jeans. Jonah bounced with excitement on the way down, bitching to William about how Yankees' games had not been available for viewing at camp.

Sam leaned against a block-long limo as they exited the hotel. The car was amazing, but so was Sam. *Looking at him never gets old.* Naomi stared through her sunglasses at him. Almost drooling, because she knew what that hard mouth could do, knew how it softened on her mouth, and sighed into her. She felt those hands, knew the strength in his arms and fingers. She knew those legs encased in faded denim, had lain between them; she slept curled against the dark hair on that chest innocently concealed beneath the virginally white T-shirt. She felt the heat of those blue eyes, those Paul Newman eyes. *I am fantasizing about him like a teenage girl!*

And in front of my son! What the hell?

Sam pushed off from the limo and opened a door for them. JoEllen waved from inside. "Hurry up, girlfriend! Let's get this show on the road." She, too, was wearing a ball cap and dark glasses.

"Sam, this is my son, Jonah Bregman. Jonah, this is Mr. Rhodes." Sam extended his hand solemnly to Jonah, who hesitated then clasped Sam's hand in a poor excuse for a handshake. Naomi's cheeks burned at the implied insult from Jonah.

"Thanks so much for including us, Mr. Rhodes." She stammered, embarrassed by her son's attitude.

"Y'all just call me Sam," he answered in an elaborate drawl. "Let's get going, Just hop in there with JoEllen and Tommy."

Jonah started to get in the car but Sam's hand on his shoulder abruptly stopped him.

"Ladies first, Jonah."

Jonah stared at him for a long moment, then dropped back. Sam smiled and offered Naomi his hand. She was shaking as she slid her hand into his. It was so warm and reassuringly hard. Jonah tumbled in behind her with Sam and William following.

The trip to Baltimore flew by as Sam chatted easily with everyone. Jonah's interest in the gadgets in the car and William's willingness to let him fool with one of the cameras lightened his mood. Camden Yards appeared too soon for Naomi, caught as she was in Sam's spell and grateful for a respite from the tension with Jonah. They pulled into a private lot. An eager young woman escorted them into the stadium, voicing her surprise that they were not in VIP seats.

"Now, ma'am, if you put us in those fancy seats, everyone would be looking at us to see if we were *famous* or *important*. We just want to relax and enjoy the game."

"You'll be recognized wherever you sit, Mr. Rhodes," she responded enthusiastically.

"No, ma'am, with this baseball cap and these shades, I'll just pass as another annoying Yankees fan. We'll find our seats by ourselves, no need to draw any attention. But, please tell Mr. Steinbrenner we appreciate the tickets."

Sam was right. They found themselves along the third base line, good seats, but not the more obvious ones behind home plate. With their Yankees caps, they endured some razzing from the Orioles fans surrounding them, but no one realized the hottest singer in country music was lounging there in the sun, his arm across the back of Naomi's seat, his other hand wrapped around a cold beer, that he barely sipped. If his fingers tangled into her loose curls no one noticed, not even her sometimes-sullen son.

Sam's eyes narrowed behind his glasses as he watched Jonah and Naomi. The boy had a chip on his shoulder as big as a house, and he was pissed at his mom. Even his excitement over being at the game couldn't quite loosen the hold his anger had on him. *Poor kid, he doesn't want to hate her but his dad's not around to take the heat. And poor Naomi, trying so hard to shield her son from an unloving father. Been there, done that.*

After a close win by the Bronx Bombers, they all tumbled back into the limo, a little sunburned and a lot stuffed with hotdogs and ice cream. After casting a furtive glance at Sam, Jonah waited for JoEllen and Naomi to enter the car before he clambered in. The car had barely left the city before Jonah was asleep, his head against Naomi's soft shoulder.

"It was a nice day, Sam, thank you," she whispered to him. JoEllen and William were at the far end of the limo. Tommy was already chattering into his cell phone. Sam stroked a finger down her cheek.

"No need for thanks, darlin'. We had a free afternoon, and I figured you were gonna have your hands full with your boy. That's one big mess of angry aimed directly at you."

"He's disappointed with David, who could blame him? So he'll take it out on me. David is never around, and when he is, nothing sticks to him. Jonah worships him." She leaned slightly toward Sam, taking care not to disturb the sleeping boy.

Sam could see the way of it. His own mother had often stood between him and his dad, but she wouldn't speak against his father. Sam deeply resented her failure to be on his side. It wasn't until later he realized the difficult position both of her men had placed her in. *Too late to let her know, too late to make it up to her.* Sometimes the bile rose up in his throat at the thought of all the opportunities he missed to do right by the women in his life.

Naomi and Sam fell into silence, both lost in their disappointments and regrets. But his hand never left hers until they pulled up in front of the hotel in the gathering dark. They rousted a sleepy Jonah; with his mother's arm around him, they shuffled through the lobby and into the elevator. With a slight kiss on Naomi's cheek, Jonah headed immediately into his bedroom as soon as they entered the suite. To Naomi's delight, the boy softly added, "Thanks, Mom," before he closed the door to his room. Blinking back tears, Naomi turned off the lights in the living room. Still warm and sticky, she started stripping off her T-shirt and jeans as soon as she got to her bedroom. After a cool shower, she, too, tumbled into bed, her mind and body exhausted from the events of the past few days.

A couple of hours later, Naomi's cell phone awakened her from her dreams of Sam. His voice was soft in her ear. "Y'all hungry?"

She yawned into the phone. "Yes, yes, I am. I thought after all we ate at the game I wouldn't be, but I now that I'm up, I'm thinking of some room service."

"Is the kid awake?" Sam's sexy growl made her shiver.

"No, he collapsed in his room with his ball and glove. Thank you so much for the baseball, Sam. I can't believe you did that!"

As they had been getting in the limo after the game, the same eager young attendant who greeted them rushed over and breathlessly informed Sam Mr. Torre wanted him to have a souvenir of the win. It was a game ball autographed by the starting line-up of the Yankees. He leaned over and gave the girl a kiss on the cheek, which prompted the "I love you, Sam" pledge from her lips. He touched her cheek and responded with his standard "I love you, too, darlin'" to the blushing young woman before he ducked into the limo.

He tossed the ball to an astonished Jonah with a wry question, "Jonah, can you hold on to this? I'd appreciate it if you would take it, I just don't have the room for it in my stuff, and anyway, I think that pitcher you like signed it." Jonah cradled the ball in his glove, through the car ride, the sleepy ascent in the elevator, and his entry into their suite.

"I've got Chinese food, darlin'. Wanna share?"

"Sure. Let me just unlock the door."

"No need," Sam laughed as he strode into her bedroom, cell phone in one hand and a steaming bag of white cartons in the other.

"How did you get in here? I meant to ask you this morning." Naomi was giggling and curious. Sam deposited the bag on her dresser and locked her door. Then he turned to drag her into his arms. After a long, deep kiss that had her head spinning, he pulled away and laughed.

"I'm starving! And I have a key." He waved it at her before he slid it back into the hip pocket of his faded jeans. Naomi scrambled up, questions and amusement in her eyes, and cleared the small table in front of the windows. *How does he do that? Put me at ease and on edge all at the same time.*

"I got the key when I booked the suite for you while you were fetching Jonah; I wanted to leave some stuff for him in his room." Sam unloaded steaming cartons of food from the brown bag.

"I didn't see anything…oh, the bag with the tour T-shirts and hats…that was from you? I thought Tommy left it. Oh, Sam." Tears filled her eyes as she hugged him hard from behind. "You really are the sweetest man!"

Sam's big hands covered hers, and he squeezed, pulling her even tighter against him. Then he turned in her arms and bent his head to kiss her. The kiss was different from all his other kisses, it was sweeter, it was softer, it almost felt like he was in love with her. Her arms tightened around him, thin bands of heat and strength holding him, pulling him in. Fatigue flowed out of her; desire took its place. She caressed the muscles bunching across his back as he held her tighter. His strong hands grasped her nightshirt and pulled it up her back, crushing the soft fabric and burning her flesh, cool in the night air, but heating from his caresses.

The nightshirt fell to floor in one swift pull. Sam backed her up against the bed; his hands were everywhere. He had not wanted her this badly before—he couldn't remember wanting any woman this much before. Her hands fumbled with his clothes; the shirt was pushed up and over. Frantic fingers worked at his jeans. "Please," he heard her whisper, "please, now, please."

Kicking out of his jeans, he freed himself, as she rolled over him. The heat at her center was burning her, igniting him. Bracing herself, hands splayed across his chest, Naomi stroked his hard length with her warm wetness, grinding into him. Throbbing slickness glided along rigid flesh. Sam groaned. "Please. You're killing me. Please." On an upward movement, she slid along his cock, then thrust back, catching him at the entrance to her heat. Down, hard and fast, until he filled her. Spasms snaked their way through her, grasping him, pulling him deeper. She rocked, once, twice. Then stopped. His eyes flew open. She smiled at him, unfathomable emotion glittering in those cat eyes. "Now," she whispered, "now."

Lost. He was lost in her. She didn't end, he didn't begin. They were one, moving as one, his hands grasping her hips; hers knotted together on his belly as she rode him, as he gave her the ride of her life. Naomi came once, pleasure playing across her face. Sam felt her release, couldn't believe she could be any wetter, any hotter. Then he surged into her, emptying himself as she whimpered, "Again and again and again," before she collapsed on top of him.

It was late when he finally left, the empty cartons scattered on the table and nightstand, sheets twisted and comforter half on the floor.

In love with her, he couldn't be in love with her. Curled up alone in the big bed, cradling the pillow that still held Sam's scent, Naomi argued with herself. Nerve endings still tingled, muscles relaxed, Naomi drifted into sleep. Sam had hugged her and kissed her goodnight, once, and then again, as if he didn't want to let her go. "Sweet dreams, love," he had whispered before he slipped silently from her room. He never used the word *love* with her before. *Could he love me? Could he? Could I?*

CHAPTER FIFTEEN

The next night it was Springsteen, the Boss, BBBRRRUUUCCEEE! The crowd at the Spectrum surged as one into a screaming stomping mass, when Sam launched into "Thunder Road," the first clue. "The best rock n' roll song ever written," Sam said, as he struck the opening chords. He made it to "I've got this guitar and I learned how to make it talk," before Springsteen strolled onto the stage and into the spot light. Naomi could feel the emotion of the crowd break over her in waves of excitement. Jonah was bouncing on his toes beside her.

Whenever Sam played "Thunder Road" on the tour, the excitement level heightened almost to the roof rafters, the buzz began, and the anticipation. You could almost hear the audience ask in one voice, *"Would Springsteen show?"* He was the one major star who had not yet appeared with Sam, and even the band was of the opinion the Boss would not make it. He had just completed over two years on the road with his own band.

Sam said nothing to anyone until that morning in Philadelphia. He and Tyrone had been in quiet conference with the sound and light techs. Jonah and her turbulent dreams were distracting Naomi.

The roadies had already taken Jonah under their wings and were letting him help set up chairs just off-stage. He had staked out his seat for the concert, stage right, just inside the curtain. Tommy had a headset on him and was letting him listen to the backstage patter of the crew and the techs. A door banged in the backstage area, followed by laughter. Deep throaty laughter and a familiar voice. Jonah just stood there, mouth agape, as The Boss sauntered by him, reaching out as he passed to give Jonah's Yankees cap a tug.

Sam strode over to Bruce, hand outstretched. They shook and then man-hugged.

"Hey, man, it is great to see you. I wasn't sure you were gonna make it."

"I told you I'd be here, but, damn, couldn't you have played somewhere in Jersey?"

"That's Tommy's doing. You'll have to take it up with him. But, hell, Jersey's just across the river, so stop your bitchin'."

The two stars laughed, as Sam punched Bruce in the shoulder. Jonah just stood there, staring, as if he could not believe that his hero was standing three feet away from him. Naomi came up behind her son, smiling at his happy face, smiling at the handsome man who had put the smile there.

"Mom, it's the Boss!" His whispered voice was full of awe and excitement.

"I know. Pretty cool, huh?" Her voice held some awe and excitement too.

"Mom, you could've told me!"

"I didn't know, Jonah. I never know who is going to appear until the day of the show. I almost cried that I missed it when Tina performed."

Jonah's mouth dropped open when Sam turned to them and motioned them over. He actually sputtered when Bruce greeted his mother with a hug that lifted her off the ground. Springsteen's Reunion tour still rated as one of Naomi's best articles; Jonah had T-shirts that were now too small from that one. But he had no idea the famous people his mom wrote about liked her. He had never been on any of the rock tours Naomi covered; he had been a little boy. And in recent years, she had only gone for a few days here and there.

The backstage came alive as the two superstars and Tyrone ran through song after song, guitars singing out "The River" and "Badlands" and Sam's classics: "Three More One Mores For the Road" and "Loose Women". William circled around them, memorializing the epic event. Even Jonah snapped dozens of pictures with one of William's back-up cameras. Naomi sat off to the side, her laptop open and her fingers flying, capturing the moment, the words practically writing themselves.

The performance of the Boss and Sam that night was the

highlight of the tour. The audience was not going to let them offstage. They played the set they rehearsed then just stopped and laughed as the audience roared, "Encore, encore!" The band finished with an impromptu version of "Jersey Girl" for Bruce's wife, Patti, who waited in the wings. Even Jonah watched in awe as his musical hero made music with his mom's newest assignment. Naomi could not be sure she heard his quiet words as the last notes sounded. "If the Boss likes Sam, maybe he isn't so bad," Jonah mused aloud, as he clapped and cheered from his seat in the shadows. "Even with all his silly rules."

No, he's not so bad, especially his silly rules. She smiled to herself as she and Jonah rose to join the crowd in its standing ovation.

CHAPTER SIXTEEN

Over the next two weeks, Naomi watched in amazement as much of Jonah's anger dissipated in the face of the good-humored ribbing from the crew, the easy acceptance from the band, and the companionship of William and Sam.

From the time Naomi started at *Rolling Stone*, shortly after her separation from David, William had been part of Naomi's extended family. Jonah was like a little brother to the talented photographer and his partner. But, William was too fun-loving and too soft-hearted to ever correct or admonish Jonah about his behavior. She had often watched William just shake his head back and forth, click his tongue, and murmur "little man, little man." When she laughed at him about his gentle admonition, William told her his grandmother had done the same to him when he acted out as a kid, and it was more effective than any slap he had received from his father. Naomi hoped Jonah would be at ease with William even in the strange atmosphere of a superstar concert tour and had counted on their easy camaraderie to ease the situation.

What had taken her by surprise was Sam. Sam spent a lot of time with Jonah, as just a friend. An older, wiser but nonjudgmental friend, too. Though Sam was strict about what he called *gentleman's rules*.

"Jonah," she had overheard Sam say a few days after her son joined them, with a bit of exaggeration in his western drawl, "my momma was the best woman I ever knew. I lost her way too soon. There is not a day I don't think about her and regret some damn fool stunt I pulled that caused her to worry or be angry. You have to treat all women with respect because that is what is right. But, you have to take extra special care of your momma. She brought you into the world."

"My mom takes care of herself," Jonah retorted. "She takes care of everything."

"Is that right?" Sam bent down to look into Jonah's eyes. "She is a mighty tough lady, that's for sure. But, she is still a little bit of a thing compared to me and you. You are already taller than her, and I'll bet you are a lot stronger."

Jonah snorted at that. "I can reach higher than her easy, and I can drag two bags to the trash and she can barely haul one."

"Then don't you think it would be a good idea for you to help her with that huge suitcase of hers? That has gotta be a real strain on her to drag that around. I swear, I don't know why women have to pack everything thing they own when they travel AND try to get it all into one bag."

"She packs way too many shoes, that's why. My mom loves shoes, Sam." The two had laughed at the vagaries of women and sauntered off together. When they got to Cleveland, Jonah pulled her suitcase off the bus and brought it up to their rooms. When she asked him if she should tip him, he had actually blushed and said, "No, Mom, it's my job as the man in the family."

Sam had only taken Jonah to task the one time in Philadelphia when he didn't hold a door for her, after that it was always *ladies first*.

Since everyone knew Naomi cursed like a sailor when riled, Sam's rule against using bad language in front of females was harder to enforce with Jonah. But, she had seen her son dutifully put a quarter in the swear jar for saying *shit* in front of Bobbi. She teased Sam about it that night as they snuggled in his bed after the concert in Toronto.

"Naomi, how am I going to get your son to clean up his dirty mouth when you let loose with the f-word at least once a day? Where did you learn to curse like that?" Sam pulled her face up from his shoulder to look at him.

"I picked it up at college. We figured if the boys could swear, so could we... You know, equal rights." Naomi laughed at the consternation in Sam's eyes.

"Well, that is not how I remember college..." at Naomi's raised eyebrow, he trailed off. "But, the air got pretty blue around the rodeos, so I guess I can't say anything to you."

"Sam, I will try to be better about it. Swearing is just a lazy use of vocabulary. And I do want Jonah to express himself without resorting to four-letter words."

Sam smiled at her but ended up turning her over his lap for a fake spanking when she added with a laugh, "I'll just teach him all the good Yiddish swear words."

Jonah also collected numerous T-shirts and ball caps from the crew and the visiting artists. The last night in Syracuse Jonah exclaimed, "My friends are going *plotz* when they see this stuff," showing the T-shirt just autographed by Hootie. And Jonah slept every night with the baseball autographed by the Yankees Sam had given him.

Her son, her laughing, sweet, funny, son was returning to her because of a bunch of good ole southern boys. She would love them all, especially Sam, for that gift alone.

CHAPTER SEVENTEEN

Saratoga Springs. Exit 13N. One mile. The green sign on the Northway flashed by the windows of Sam's bus. Naomi was excited. Excited and nervous. She had not been home in almost a year. Visits to her mother's house were difficult at best. Miriam was a caustic force of jealousy and revenge, and her mother was, well, still the peacekeeper. First, between Naomi and her father, now between Naomi and Miriam.

Jonah looked forward to some time with his *bubbe* and his cousins. Though, he had admitted early that morning as they left Syracuse he wanted to ride with the guys one last time because he was really going to miss them. So Sam and Naomi sat on his bus, just holding hands, through the late August morning.

Sam had not played the Saratoga Performing Arts Center in several years. Tickets for the concert for the next night sold out in near-record time, and the band was eager to be back in the open air amphitheater. Naomi loved SPAC. It was where she had seen her first concert…the Beach Boys. When she told Sam, he replied he was fairly certain the Beach Boys would not be the surprise guests, but maybe some local talent would appear instead. He was still pretty close-mouthed with her about who the guest stars would be at each show. Tommy said it was because they were fitting people in as their schedules allowed. Naomi thought it was part of Sam's more private nature. Either way, it contributed to the edginess of her story. Like she needed any more edginess given her continued uneasiness about her feelings for Sam.

They had been sitting in silence. Sam finally spoke as the bus pulled off the Northway and onto Route 9. He put his finger on her lower lip. Naomi knew she was chewing on it. Stressing out about introducing Sam to her mother, dealing with Miriam, leaving Jonah for the last leg of the trip. And her growing need for Sam. Sam ran a finger lightly along lips swollen from his kisses earlier in the morning. He pulled a Diet Coke out of the mini fridge near his seat.

"Drink this, Naomi, before you chew all your lip gunk right off."

She shot him a look, one of her disdainful *New York* looks. Then sighed and leaned into him. "I know, Sam, I know. I just hate having to deal with all the *mishegas.* I mean craziness, as in Miriam's craziness," she added when Sam looked confused. He already knew her older sister was a thorn in her side, constantly putting her mother between them, constantly jockeying for position in the family hierarchy. She had told him how much that frustrated her because, while Naomi had conceded the *princess* title to Miriam years before, now Miriam was doing it with the kids, too. Miriam constantly tried to make comparisons between Jonah and her daughter and son, who lived just around the corner from their grandmother.

"Don't worry, darlin'. Jonah can hold his own. He's got plenty of stories to tell his cousins, and it won't hurt we loaded him up with tour stuff to smooth the way. Besides, he told me the other day he was pretty sure his grandma loved him best because he looks the most like your father."

"I can't believe he told you that," Naomi said somewhat astonished Jonah opened up that much to Sam.

"He's not slow, you know, Naomi. Kids pick up on stuff like that real quick. And besides, he's probably right. My grandma liked me best for the same reason."

A short time later, Naomi checked into her room at the Gideon Putnam, just a short walk across the lawn to the performing arts center, even though she knew she would be staying with Sam that night. Before she could be alone with Sam, she needed go to her mother's house with Jonah. The plan was he would stay with his grandmother until his father came to take him for Labor Day.

After an early lunch and a swim in the pool, Naomi and Sam left the hotel with Jonah bouncing in the back seat of Tommy's SUV. The small brick ranch on Iroquois Drive looked exactly the same to Naomi as it had throughout her childhood. Her mother planted the same petunias every spring, the same herbs by the kitchen door, and the same vegetables crowding around the back porch. "An American house," she always said. "We live in an American house." The stars and stripes hung from the front porch, put out every morning, brought in at night. Naomi's parents had always been grateful for the home they found after the war and had always proudly demonstrated their love for their new country.

But inside the house was a mix of Europe and America, religious and secular, old and new. There was a *mezuzah* hanging on the doorframe into almost every room, but there was a new flat screen TV in the living room so her mother could watch her shows—every crime drama on every channel. Lilli Stein loved them because the bad guys always got caught. Not at all like her own childhood when the bad guys killed almost every person she loved. Framed prints of the Old Masters hung in the dining room, next to framed pictures of George W. Bush and Golda Meir. State of the art appliances stood shining in the kitchen, but tea was still drunk out of tall glasses with a silver spoon and a cube of sugar.

Her mother's voice rang down the narrow hall from the kitchen. "*Ketzela*, is that you? Is my *shayna punim* with you?" Lilli came around the corner, wiping her hands on her apron.

"There, *bubele,* there is my fine boy. *Oy*, you've grown again!" Her mother, trim and tiny still, held out her arms to them. Naomi felt a lump in her throat as her mother caressed her cheek with one hand and rubbed Jonah's head with the other. *It is good to be home.*

Sam stood by the front door. Naomi had been reluctant to let him come over, but he had insisted, laughingly asserting she had already met his whole family: Bobbi. Lilli Stein took one look at him and said, "Come. You'll eat." And, "I like your songs," before turning and following Jonah back to the kitchen, where he erupted in cheers of delight when he saw the food spread out on his grandmother's table.

"We don't have to," Naomi told him. "You can go back if you want." Her mother's background sometimes made outsiders uncomfortable. Sam moved past her on his way to the kitchen saying, "Are you kidding? This smells as good as Rosie's place!"

The evening was lovely. Sam's eyes glowed as Naomi and her mother covered their heads and lit the Shabbes candles, their two voices a sweet harmony as they sang the prayers. Naomi even said a few lines of *Eshet Chayil*, "A Woman of Valour", explaining to Sam her father had said the words to her mother every Friday night.

A woman of valour who can find? For her price is far above rubies.

The heart of her husband doth safely trust in her, and he hath no lack of gain.

She doeth him good and not evil all the days of her life….

Two hours followed with Mrs. Stein fussing with the food and Jonah spilling tales of the tour and crumbs from his mouth at the same time. The dreaded Miriam did not arrive, and all was peaceful, if not quiet. As she passed between table and stove, counter and refrigerator, Lilli's hands never failed to pat Jonah's head or squeeze Naomi's shoulder. Eventually, she even laid a gnarled hand on Sam's arm as she urged him to *essen, essen*—eat, eat.

Darkness was all around them, with the sounds of small town America whispering up and down the quiet street as they left the house. Lilli insisted they take a box of rugelach and a loaf of fresh challah to see them through the weekend.

"She reminds me of my mother, with her peaceful smile and watchful eyes," Sam told Naomi as they climbed into Tommy's Navigator. "Mom always worried that I didn't eat enough."

"I know what you mean. She is like the universal mom." Naomi leaned in to kiss him on the cheek in a moment of shared thankfulness for mothers and their unquestioning love. Later that evening, lying in bed at the Gideon, they talked about mothers and fathers, children, dreams and hopes and disappointments. They were tired and replete after their dinner at Lilli's house followed by drinks at The Parting Glass and skulking around Saratoga in disguise. The Track was open, the streets downtown filled with people laughing or sighing over the day's race results. They found anonymity in the crowd and loved it.

But now was the time for cuddles and caresses and conversation. Naomi sipped from the glass of wine they shared. Propped against pillows cushioning the ornate headboard, Sam draped across the foot of the bed, rubbing her feet, Naomi opened up the history of her family for him.

"My parents were not even teenagers when they were sent to the camps. They survived Auschwitz only to lose their entire families. After the war, they spent years in Displaced Persons camps in Europe. They met in a DP camp and fell in love, or in need. They had no one else, nothing to their names, except what they got from the Red Cross. The US wasn't even letting displaced persons into the country until 1947. There were so many restrictions; you couldn't get in unless you had a sponsor, and it was difficult to reach out to family in America from those camps. My father had been so young when the Nazis invaded and sent his family to Auschwitz. He could barely remember the names of family members who had emigrated to America way before the war. Finally, my grandfather's cousins tracked him down. They ran a pharmacy here in Saratoga. My parents were married by then. The cousins brought them over and sent my father to school. He became a pharmacist like them. He was so strong, much stronger than my mom in so many ways. He acclimated faster than she did. My mother always wanted to be a doctor, like her father, but she never went to school after Auschwitz, except for some classes in the DP camps. After she married my dad, she wanted to just stay in the house and make a home. She was so dependent on my dad for everything for so long. Her adventurous spirit was destroyed by the Nazis. But, she wanted to be a good American, so she read and read and learned English and American History. They both became citizens as soon as they could."

Naomi sighed and Sam wiped the single tear from her cheek. It was a sad story, common to thousands. "I know the history, Naomi, but I never really understood until I met you and your mother. I had never seen the numbers on anyone's arm until tonight. Your mother is a very courageous woman." Sipping from the glass of wine, Naomi continued to speak softly. "She never wears a sleeveless dress or blouse, no matter the temperature. And when strangers are around she always wears long sleeves. She has to feel really comfortable with someone to roll up her sleeves, even a little, like she did tonight when she was doing the dishes." Naomi smiled sadly at Sam before she continued.

"It took some years before my mother could have children, she was so malnourished from the war and the camps. They tried and tried. Miriam was born first and they named her for my father's mother. My father wanted a son to carry on the family name— there was no one left but him of his entire branch of the family. My mom had several miscarriages and then I came along. My father was so disappointed after I was born to learn my mother couldn't have any more children. By the time I was five, I knew my father had no use for me. I tried to please him, but I looked too much like the sister who was killed in the camps, the one I was named for. That hurt him. I was a constant reminder of what he lost. And, I wasn't a boy, even though I was a tomboy. I just wasn't the son he hoped for. He constantly criticized me for not being a little lady like Miriam. He was so distant from me. That just made Miriam so happy. So I guess I was closer to my mom. But she was caught between me and my father, and my father always won. God, it was so hard to be here in those days, nothing I did was right!"

"I know what that's like," Sam spoke softly. "It is as if you lived parts of my life. My father wanted me to be everything he could not be in high school and college. He had been a good athlete, but I was better. He was so competitive at sports, and I just liked being with my friends on the team. I mean, I wanted to win, but winning wasn't everything like it was for him. The last years I lived home, we fought all the time. It was hell on my mom. He was better when I went to college, played football, scored touchdowns. He wanted me to turn pro when I graduated. And I thought about that, even though I really didn't want a career in the NFL. Then, when I blew my knee out riding broncos the summer of my junior year and lost my football scholarship, he practically disowned me."

Naomi rubbed Sam's leg where the faded scars crisscrossed from mid-thigh to mid-calf. "Sam you don't have to talk about him if it bothers you so much. I can see how much it still hurts you to talk about your dad. Bobbi told me you all never really mended the fences broken between you before he died."

"It's all right, darlin'. I want you to know about me." Sam moved from the foot of the bed, to put his arm around Naomi. Leaning back against the pillows, he pulled her close before he continued. "I always wanted to make music, and I thought if I became a success, he might finally accept me and be proud of me again. I pushed too hard after college; I had promised Emily I would only try for a little while, but things were happening for the band, slowly, but I was sure we would make it, I was so sure. I just stayed out on the road."

The words started to come slower then, as Sam forced himself to tell Naomi the rest of his story. About Emily and how she lost a baby when he was on the road.

"I didn't get back to her in time, and she had had to have an emergency hysterectomy to repair the damage. I wasn't there for her, and she had always been there for me. I promised her I would stay home and quit the band. She wouldn't hear of that. Even though it cost her our baby, she didn't ask me to give up the band. She gave me up instead."

"Oh, Sam. You poor things. You and Emily, you lost a child, and then you lost each other. That is so sad. I can't even imagine. I lost David, but I kept Jonah. I don't know what I would do if I lost him, too."

Sam rested his chin on top of Naomi's tangled curls. He had not spoken about his parents or his tangled love life with anyone in years. Not since tequila and guilt forced him to spill the secrets of his soul to Tyrone and Tommy in the mountains of Colorado. It hurt to reveal himself to Naomi, but he knew now she was a kindred spirit. The words came faster as he resumed his story.

"I wasn't really with Lola until after Emily told me she was divorcing me. Bobbi was off having her first baby, and Lola stepped in for her. But we had been flirting on the road, and when I came back after Emily, Lola was ready to welcome me with open arms. It was a mistake, but I didn't see it. I thought I could have with Lola what I lost with Emily. I could have a wife who toured with me, we could bring our kids on the road with us. It can be done." He squeezed Naomi's hand hard as though he was trying to reassure himself he had been right.

"But she left me when I pressed her about starting a family. It wasn't because she was pissed about the Garth-Trisha song." Naomi pulled her head off his shoulder and gave him a look that said she was not convinced about his version of the story. Sam shook his head.

"It was me. I was so sure I could make it work with her, I pushed her to get pregnant. Well, you saw her. She's younger than me, and she puts so much value on her looks, even though she doesn't need to. You heard her sing."

Naomi nodded her agreement. "Lola *can* sing, Sam, but she is vain and self-centered. And calculating. I know all about that. She is exactly the kind of woman David left me for: younger, sexier, same profession." Kissing Sam's shoulder, Naomi continued. "I know all about taking the blame for other's actions, I've been doing it for years with David and Jonah. I am going to stop doing that. It doesn't help Jonah, and it hurts me. You should try it."

He laughed bitterly at her words. "We'll see. But, I can't fix Lola now. I pushed too hard, and she pulled away. I pushed harder, and I told her that I was thinking of stopping the tour so we could sort it out. Seems it was the tour that she wanted, not me. She left the next day. So, I'm not taking the blame for her leaving. But I blame myself for believing she loved me. Enough." He said it with a self-mocking chuckle.

Then, he quieted. Pulling her tightly into his arms, Sam spoke softly about Beckie, also younger but not in the business. She joined the tour to handle wardrobe, hair, and make-up for Bobbi and JoEllen. He had not noticed her at first in those months after Lola when he flitted from woman to woman, a different one in every town they played. But that got old fast, and once he sobered up a bit and slowed down, he noticed the quiet, sandy-haired girl with the golden freckles, violet eyes and wide, open smile. Sam smiled, too, as he recalled his late wife.

"She was so in love with *Sam the man*, not *Sam the star*. I could do no wrong in her eyes. As much as she loved the music, the band, and the traveling, she didn't mind being home when she was pregnant with Sarah. She just wanted to be with me and the family we were building. Beckie even came back out on the road for a bit after the baby came. Those were the best days. Sarah was…so…special."

His voice cracked. Naomi reached out to him. "Oh, Sam, you loved them so much. I am so sorry you lost them."

Sam didn't say very much about the death of his third wife and daughter, only that he had gone out on one more tour date when he should have stayed home with Sarah and Beckie. "So, sweet thing, it looks like I am damaged goods. I am just a curse on a good woman. Maybe it's for the better, maybe I would be just as bad a father as my dad." He laughed bitterly and drained the glass of wine. Sam's lips brushed her hair before he reached out to turn off the light. It was quiet and dark in their room, but it was a long time before either of them fell asleep. They stayed in each other's arms through the night.

The next day flew by in a flurry of activity. Early in the morning, Sam insisted on going to WGNA for a surprise visit with Shawn and Ritchie on their new morning show They were thrilled to see him and surprised he was with a *hometown girl*. After the interview and some good-natured fooling around, Sam and Naomi picked up Jonah at Lilli's and made their way down Route 9 to SPAC. Rehearsals were easy and loose, considering Dave Mathews was the guest star. Although he performed his annual two-night gig in Saratoga in July, Dave returned for Sam. Naomi was no longer surprised at the affection and admiration other performers, both young and old, had for Sam. She felt it too.

Later that night, you couldn't hear a note when Dave Mathews sauntered on-stage to sing "Crash" with Sam. As loud as it had been during their duet, the amphitheater virtually exploded when Sam did the "Dixie Chicken" solo. The song was perfect for Sam. In the wings, even Jonah sang along. He leaned into his mom, laughing and smiling, her little boy again. Naomi hugged him hard, and he didn't even squirm away. He wore the T-shirt Sam had gotten him from Dave Mathews, and the camera William gave him that morning around his neck. Perched back to front on his head was one of Sam's old University of Oklahoma baseball caps. Jonah was in his glory! And Naomi's heart melted.

CHAPTER EIGHTEEN

The last concert date was Salt Lake City; a two-week break in the tour followed. After a wild night with Steven Tyler, the band was ready for some time off. And so was Naomi. She said as much to William as she saw him off at the airport. "I'm too old for this shit." She practically moaned the words while she hugged his bony frame.

William just grinned and said "You know you love it! You haven't looked this good in years, girlfriend. Touring, or maybe something else, just makes you glow." Naomi swatted his behind as he gathered up his backpack and gear and headed off on his long-delayed trip to Morocco.

Everyone else scattered to homes and families, scheduled to meet back in New York City in September. Naomi planned to fly home to New York and take Jonah to Cape Cod for Labor Day, as David had once again reneged on his promise of time with his son. But even though David failed to include Jonah in the much promised vacation in the Hamptons, Jonah told her he was happy to stay in Saratoga with his grandmother and assorted cousins. From Salt Lake City, Naomi and Jonah had a long talk about David's latest failure as a father.

"Mom, I'm done with him," Jonah stated firmly. "I am not going to wait for him to decide he wants to be my father. He doesn't love me."

Naomi started to protest to her son, but stopped. "He loves you, Jonah, just not as much as he loves himself. He will always do what he wants, he always has. If it hurts you, he regrets it—just not enough to change his ways. I am so sorry."

"Don't apologize for him anymore. Mom, you do that all the

time. He isn't worth it." Her son sighed into the phone.

"No, he is not worthy of a son like you, Jonah. It is his loss." Naomi's heart broke at this sad truth, but Jonah was becoming a young man, and it was time to stop taking the blame for David. Maybe her ex-husband would one day realize what he lost when he turned his back on Jonah. But, for now, it would be just Jonah and Naomi.

"Hey, Mom, don't worry about me. I'm having a good time at Bubbe's, and we're all going to the Track this week and to the Great Escape, too." He learned a lot this summer about responsibility from the guys on the tour, especially Sam and Tyrone. "I'll see you next week at home. *Y'all* have a good time with Sam." They hung up laughing.

Naomi related the conversation to Sam the next day as they rode in the Hummer limousine from the Denver airport to his ranch, after their short flight from Utah. She marveled at Jonah's newfound maturity. Sam laughed and said, "Yeah, take a boy on the road for a few weeks, and he turns into a man. It's all the lifting and pulling that must do it. That or the girlie magazines in the crew's bus!"

"Sam, stop, it must have been something that happened on the tour. Maybe it was hanging around with you."

Sam's guffaw filled the car. "I'm no one's good example, darlin'. Never have been, never will be."

Early in the afternoon, the Hummer cruised down a long single lane to a sprawling ranch house, nestled in a small valley in the San Juan Mountains. Naomi could see there were horses and livestock, in the fenced areas in the distance, behind a barn and various outbuildings. Sam was twitchy in the seat beside her, his movements giving away his happiness at being home and his anticipation about her reaction. Maria and Hosea, the elderly couple who worked on the spread before Sam bought it, stood on the wide front veranda waving as the car approached. Sam greeted them warmly, in Spanish, and their affection for him was evident on their faces and the hugs they gave him. A speculative glance passed between them when Sam introduced Naomi and said she would be staying with him for the next week and preparing the guest suite would not be necessary.

Sam escorted Naomi through the house. "I sort

of…retreated…here after Beckie and Sarah passed. I guess I went a little crazy with the construction and all, but it seemed that when I was busy building, I didn't drink as much, and I didn't have time to dwell on what happened to them." They took a turn out of the living room with its two-story stone fireplace and wall of glass into what was obviously a new addition to the structure. "I added on a new master bedroom suite. It faces to the west. I wanted unobstructed views of the mountains; I needed to be able to see them when I woke up. The old master bedroom is on the other side of the house. I converted it into a guest suite, and turned Sarah's bedroom into an office." They were back in the living room, Sam gesturing down another hall. "The recording studio is this way. Tyrone and Tommy, once I finally let them in, helped with expanding that area, and adding some newer equipment. I swear I never thought to pick up a guitar again after…Oklahoma. They saved me. They really saved me."

Naomi turned to give him a bear hug that almost knocked him over. "I'm glad they did, Sam. I am so glad they did." It was impossible not to fall in love with the majestic landscape, Naomi thought; so much more rugged and grand than her Adirondacks. She loved, too, the peace and the beauty of the house, filled with regional art and furniture. And she was touched by Sam's pride as he showed her around. "I love it, Sam! It is beautiful and it is *so* you. You should be so proud of all of this." He picked her up and swung her around, grinning.

Sam insisted on showing her some of the property as soon as she changed. Naomi gingerly climbed on the dappled mare Sam saddled for her. She rode in Saratoga in her youth, but she had not been on a horse for several years. *My thighs are going to be like jelly tonight*. Fortunately, Sam took pity on her and did not take her much beyond sight of the house.

Sam and Naomi returned to the ranch for a swim in the natural stone pool. Dripping water, they bundled up the spicy meal left warming for them by Maria, grabbed some Coronas, and retreated to the master suite—with its huge bed, natural woven throws and pillows, and free-form fireplace. Laying a woven blanket in front of the fire, Sam made a picnic while Naomi dried off in the master bath. She emerged to the cozy scene, wrapped in an old robe Sam loaned her—and her turquoise moccasins.

"Naomi, those are the most ridiculous shoes! I am going to take you into town tomorrow to get some new ones. Those are falling apart!" He patted the blanket next to him and handed her a beer.

"Great! But only if they're turquoise." She laughed at him as she sank down beside him. "They're my good luck slippers. Remember Bozeman?"

His gut tightened at the memory of her tongue on him and then her legs wrapped around him. "Yeah," he growled, "I remember Bozeman. Do you remember Chicago?"

She quivered at his words; Sam put his beer down and reached for hers. After placing them carefully out of range, he pulled Naomi into his arms. His mouth fell on hers, forcing her lips open with his tongue and his teeth. He devoured her, his tongue sweeping past her teeth, swirling through her mouth, drinking her as if he were a man dying of thirst. She clung to his shoulders, whimpering with passion.

Sam's mouth broke away from Naomi's, trailing hot kisses across her jaw and down to her shoulders. She wrapped her arms tight around his neck, pressing up into him, plastered against him, trying to get inside him.

He was hungry, hungry for her. It slammed into him, even as he tried to control his ardor. He was so hard it hurt, throbbing, ready to explode. *Slow down, slow down.* But his hands were inside her robe, pulling it apart and off her shoulders, as his mouth descended on her breasts.

Naomi cried out as his teeth fastened on her nipple and he sucked. She bucked against him, trying to reach him, but her arms were pinned inside the folds of the robe. Bent over his arm, breasts bared in the flickering firelight, bathed in its soft glow, she looked like a pagan sacrifice in an erotic ritual of surrender. He ravished her with his mouth and teeth and hands, breathing her in, devouring first one nipple than the other.

Sam feasted on her flesh, his mouth everywhere, his hands holding her and molding her flesh into receptacles for his kisses. He moved lower, his tongue curling into her navel on his journey to her core. Writhing, Naomi wiggled her arms out of the sleeves just as he dipped his head between her legs. Reaching out for him, he thwarted her attempts to pull him up for a kiss when he slipped his fingers into her. She fell back, neck limp but torso quivering.

Looking up, Sam's breath caught. *Right now, right here, she is everything. Everything I want and need.*

"God, Naomi, you are so hot. So hot and so sweet." It was too much, too much, fingers sliding into her wet heat, his mouth eating at her, sucking her until she thrashed and moaned like a wanton.

"Go, Naomi, go over. Come for me, come for me." His urgent words tore at her.

She raised her head, licked her lips, and looked at him through half-closed eyes. She watched him watching her, watched his head lower, watched his tongue flick out in a long stroke over her throbbing bud. She never watched him before, but now she couldn't seem tear her eyes away.

Eyes locked on her eyes, he feasted on her. Her lips parted, she dragged air into her lungs, in panting breaths, as she gathered herself for the coming onslaught of pleasure. Her eyes closed as her hips began to piston against his mouth. Her hands found his hair and held him there, *just there*, as she came and came.

Before the last spasm echoed through her, Sam lifted her in his arms for a wet kiss. Limp arms held him as she feasted on his mouth and her taste. He flipped her then. To her surprise, she was on her stomach, and he was lifting her to her knees. Naomi's tangled curls, golden in the dying light, fell forward, draping her shoulders and arms. He pulled her to him, fitting himself between her legs. Rising on her elbows, she flung her hair to one side and looked back at him.

"Just like Chicago?" She laughed weakly.

"Are you up to it?" He paused, his hands on her hips.

"I'll kill you if you don't come inside me right now." Naomi arched her back.

Yes. Sam's hardness pushed between her legs, finding her wetness, her heat. She pushed back against him until he buried his cock in her. Then she began to move, circling her hips, as his thrusts went deeper and deeper.

"Darlin', you are not going to have to kill me. I think I'm dying, dying from having you." As if inflamed by his words, Naomi squeezed him tightly with her inner muscles, clenching to keep him from pulling all the way out. Then the spasms started again deep inside her. His hands tightened on her hips as he pumped into her, emptied into her. Sated, they collapsed in front of the fire, wrapped in the soft blankets and each other. Later, much later, they awoke to nibble on their dinner and crawl into the big bed.

In the morning, Naomi awakened first. Sore but so satisfied, she stretched, easing away from Sam's embrace. He slept on, the ravages of weeks on the road almost erased by one day and one night at his retreat. Naomi wrapped a multi-colored throw around her naked body and climbed out of bed. After sneaking into the bathroom for two Tylenol and a quick brushing of her teeth, she moved to the alcove across from the bed. She stood, looking out at the sunrise breaking over the mountains, reflected off the pool. The blue sky was shot with yellow and orange, crimson and purple in the shadows. The clouds were thin strands of silver. The air was cool and still, broken only by the cries of a hawk wheeling above the trees at the end of the drive. Naomi was awestruck by the beauty and grandeur spread out before her.

Sam threw the covers back from the bed. The soft whoosh and thump of the blankets hitting the floor interrupted Naomi's thoughts. She turned and saw him, as if for the first time. Naked, he appeared bronzed in the sunlit shadows, tall and strong, the scars on his knee and ribs stark in the reflected light, the silver in his black hair glistening, his blue eyes dark and unreadable.

Mindful of the words from Shakespeare, *what a piece of work is man*, she murmured the lines out loud.

He smiled and stepped up to enfold her, wrapping her in his embrace, burying his face in her hair. Encircled by Sam's arms, Naomi felt complete, finally at peace. The beauty of the morning, the night of loving before, and Sam's protective stance broke the final hold on her heart.

I love him. God help me, I love him.

Her heart opened to him. She whispered "I love you, Sam."

He stiffened momentarily, but then his arms tightened around her, and he said quickly, "I love you, too, darlin'."

Sam's casual reply pierced Naomi's heart. She was lost. He had said the same thing, in exactly the same way, a hundred times, to fans, to the crew, to other artists. When met with the constant statements of love from people, "I love you, Sam" they would confess, in whispers or in screams, he always replied, quickly and smoothly, "I love you, too, darlin'."

Naomi turned in his arms and stared up at him.

"Say it again, Sam."

"Say what?"

"Say you love me."

Looking uncomfortable, Sam's eyes shifted away from her, just for a second, before he said it again. Before he said, "I love you too, darlin'." In that same automatic, detached way he had said it a million times before. His blue eyes cooled, flattened, and his lips curved into his sardonic *Sam* grin.

Naomi turned away from him, not sure what her response should be. He had just broken her heart. She could not believe she even offered her badly damaged heart to him, surprised she could feel anything like the love she felt for him. But she was not settling again, she wanted the whole *megillah* or nothing at all. Straightening her shoulders, she took a deep breath and said, "I need to get back to New York. I can't stay beyond today." She stepped away from him. Sam stiffened at her words. He reached for her but she shrugged him away. If he touched her, she would break.

"Sam, I have to get this story written, and I still have my commitment to the Liebowitz book. I have a life and I need to get back to it."

He just stared at her.

"I thought we had something."

Naomi paused hoping he was finally going to say *I love you*. Like he meant it. She was waiting for something. Something important.

"What is it we had, Sam?"

"I thought we were good together. You fit me like a glove. I want more time with you. I thought you wanted more time with me." The words sounded stilted and false.

He still couldn't tell her he loved her. Naomi realized he had no idea what he had done—he probably didn't even realize he told her he loved her the same way he told the attendant at the Yankees' game or the waitress at Rosie's or a thousand others. *Maybe he couldn't say it because he was still in love with Beckie.*

"I need to shower." Naomi walked into the bathroom and closed the door.

Finding herself in an empty room when she emerged from the bathroom, she realized the hot steamy water had done little to ease the ache in her muscles and nothing for the ache in her heart, Naomi threw her cosmetic case into her open suitcase and dressed quickly. *If he can just turn away from me, there's nothing for me here. I might as well leave today.* She picked up the phone on the nightstand to call the airport.

As he had done after the deaths of his wife and daughter, Sam retreated to his studio. Naomi's business-like words had punched him in his gut. Her statement and her plans for an imminent departure stunned him. He thought they would have a several days together before she left and the tour resumed.

Hadn't she just said she loved me? Didn't I say I loved her too? What was wrong with her? She was being a hard-assed reporter again. Maybe he had pegged her right when he first met her. All *New York* and all business.

Then he remembered how she looked that morning. He had awakened quietly not wanting to disturb her rest, but she was gone from his bed. He looked toward the light and there she was. She stood in front of the window, in stark contrast to the still dark mountains spread out before her, the gold highlights in her hair shimmering from the sun's rays creeping over the peaks. Taken by her beauty, her strength, and her fragility, Sam felt his heart move, opening a bit to this beautiful vibrant woman. Then hurt shimmered through him. *No. It was too painful.* He shook off memories of the happy times he once had at the ranch and the heartache he came here to escape. *Too much, too much. I can't feel this much again. Slow down. Back off.*

He was drawn to her nonetheless and had risen to bring her back to bed. He was totally unprepared for her declaration of love. So, he'd manned up and said the right thing. But, it wasn't enough for her. Guilt pierced his soul; she had looked so fragile, her words so wistful, when she asked him to tell her what it was that they had. *Well, I told her. I guess it just wasn't good enough for her. It will have to be, at least for now. I am giving her all I've got in me.* She'll have to accept that. With the situation resolved in his mind, Sam turned on the concert recordings and lost himself and his worries in the music.

When Sam finally cleared the songs from his head, he went looking for Naomi. Not finding her in the bedroom or guest suite or living room, he cornered Maria in the kitchen.

"Señora Naomi left two hours ago. She said she had to get a flight back to New York." Maria was wiping her hands, trying not to look at Sam's face, pity in every glance she gave him. It was a shot to his gut. *Jesus, I was right. She played me.*

"Yeah, I guess she got what she came for." His words were as harsh and cold

"What was that, Señor Sam?"

"A story, Maria. Just a story."

CHAPTER NINETEEN

Naomi sat huddled in first class, for the entire flight, berating herself for once again loving a man who couldn't—or wouldn't—love her back. Like David. Like her father. Her eyes swollen and her stomach queasy, it was the worst flight of her life. Tired and worn out, she collapsed in her dusty and stuffy apartment, ignoring her mail, her phone, and her computer. For two days, she moved from the bed to the bathroom and back, sleeping restlessly until nausea awakened her. *Dammit! I couldn't catch the man, but I had to catch some damn end of summer flu!*

The arrival of Jonah a few days after her return lifted her spirits but did nothing for Naomi's tired bones and rebellious stomach.

"Mom, I have to say it, you look like the east end of a horse heading west!"

"Jonah, that is *not* funny! Couldn't you have picked up a more polite cowboy saying?"

"Tyrone says it all the time, Mom. And you really liked him." Jonah was grinning at her, as he brought crackers and ginger ale.

"Yes, I did. Tyrone is a real country gentleman." Naomi's smile brightened her wan face.

"You liked Sam even better, Mom." Jonah was watching her closely.

Naomi started to protest but remembering her promise to stop sugarcoating life's bumps and bruises, she replied, "Yes, I did, Jonah. I liked Sam a lot. And he liked me. Just not enough."

Reaching out to hug her, Jonah said softly, "I like you enough, Ema. I love you enough."

"Oh, Jonah, I love you too. More than enough, more than anything!" She held her precious son in her arms.

And she started to heal with that quiet profession of love from her son. *At least I have my child.*

One week later, those words came back to haunt her.

"A child! Are you crazy! How can I be pregnant? I'm on the pill!" Naomi was fuming. Her OB/GYN just grinned at her.

"Well, at least you're not going to try to tell me that you haven't had sex!" Dr. Rosen had been pushing her for years to get back into dating or, as he said, "get back in the saddle." He would laugh even harder if she told him that was exactly what had gotten her into this predicament. "You know the pill is only about ninety-nine percent effective. Where do you think the other one percent comes from…the stork?" He laughed and patted her shoulder. But, later when they conferred in his office, he was full of concern and directions, scheduling appointments and writing prescriptions. "We'll get you through it, Naomi, don't worry. You'll be laughing about all this someday."

Walking out of the office, Naomi did not think her predicament was funny. Not by a long shot. *Single and pregnant at thirty-six.* What was she going to do? Almost as soon as the question formed, the answer came. She would raise this baby. Her job was flexible and she could easily afford to care for her child. Her hand rested on her abdomen as she went into the pharmacy to pick up her prenatal vitamins. But she would need some help.

The next day, Naomi called Jonah's school and told them that he would not be attending until after the Jewish holidays; family business required his presence in Saratoga Springs. It was not a problem in New York City with so many schools giving students time off for Rosh Hashanah and Yom Kippur. The school would e-mail lessons to Jonah he could turn in when he returned. Naomi let Jed and Janice know she was going to her mother's to recuperate from her flu ordeal. On September 9, she packed Jonah into a rented convertible and drove to Saratoga. Arriving late in the evening, Naomi practically collapsed in her mother's arms. After a good meal, and ten hours of sleep in her old bed, she felt marginally human again. Her mother made French toast and lemon tea for breakfast. After he had eaten, Jonah was shooed out of the kitchen by his bubbe.

"So," said Lilli Stein as she poured more hot water into her daughter's glass of tea. Naomi looked over at her mother, seated

adjacent to her at the old oak kitchen table in the sunny breakfast
nook off the kitchen. Her mother idly stirred the silver spoon in her
glass of golden tea. Then she simply smiled and waited. She had
the patience of the ages, the patience of someone who waited
through years in a concentration camp and then years in a
Displaced Persons camp. She could wait forever.

"So," Naomi responded with a sigh. "I messed up, Ema. I
messed up big time."

"We can work it out, Naomi. There is nothing God sends us that
we cannot deal with if we pray and think." Lilli reached out and
squeezed her daughter's hand. That was all it took for the tears to
start oozing out of Naomi's eyes and dripping down her cheeks. It
had been a long time, a very long time, since Naomi had cried to
her mother. Lilli pulled a handkerchief from the pocket of her
housecoat and wiped at the tears. "There, there, *shayna*. What is
wrong? I will help you."

"I'm pregnant. And Sam doesn't love me, really. And I'm
scared and angry and happy and sad and embarrassed all at the
same time. I don't know what to do, Ema." Naomi sniffled then
blew her nose in her mother's soft, faded hankie. "No, I do know
one thing: I am going to keep this baby."

"Of course you are." Her mother sounded outraged at the notion
that Naomi would do anything else. "Does Jonah know?"

"He does. And he says he is okay with it. He was surprised but
not angry and not ashamed of me. He does think I should tell Sam,
though."

Lilli smiled a tentative smile. "What do you think, my girl?"

"At first I was adamant that I would not tell him. But, now, I
think he deserves to know. I don't expect anything from him, but I
think he would want to know." Naomi looked miserably out the
window at the sunny day. She felt far removed from the warm
light.

"Naomi, what happened with you and Sam? Everything was
wonderful and then it was not."

"I told him I loved him and I do...did. He just gave me the same
line he says to everyone... 'I love you, too, darlin'...' He couldn't
just say "I love you." Maybe he can't love anyone anymore, but I
am not going to wait around and find out I am not the one for him.
Not like David. It's all or nothing. I am not going to beg another

man to love me. Been there, done that…twice." Naomi pressed her lips together and tossed her blond hair defiantly.

Lilli exhaled a tired sigh. "Naomi, David left you and he was wrong to do that, wrong to get involved with a much younger *shiksa* who worked for him, no less. I don't think any of us saw really how self-centered and how controlling he could be. You were so determined to have a life of your own and a love of your own, even if we had warned you, you would not have listened to us. But, you did that partly because of your father. You never understood him."

Naomi stopped her mother with a raised hand. "Mom. No excuses. He's gone, and you can stop making excuses for him. Especially now. I don't need to hear how I was not enough for my husband to love and not enough for my father to love. And I am not enough for Sam to love either. I am just not enough." Hiccupping sobs choked off her angry words.

"I make no excuses for David, my dear. But I will speak for your father. He loved you from the moment you were born. Yes, he was disappointed you were not a boy. With his entire family destroyed by the Nazis, he so wanted his name to be carried on, to be remembered, not just for his sake, but for the sake of his family. But he loved you. He carried you and tucked you in; he was always the one who pushed your stroller. It was only when you got to be three or four, and you looked just like his little sister, her name should be a blessing. You looked just like Naomi at the same age, at the age those monsters took her, the last time he saw her. That is when he pulled back, Naomi. You had her name and her face and seeing you was just like having her here again. And he was so afraid of losing you, of losing his little sister again, he tried to save his heart, tried not to love you so if you were taken, his heart would not break again. He was not sure he could survive such a loss."

Lilli's voice faded. She sighed and her strong shoulders slumped, just a bit, before she straightened and looked her daughter in the eyes. "He loved you. But he was damaged by the war, and in turn, he damaged you. Not all our wounds are visible, Naomi. You can see some of mine. But your father…his wounds were buried deep inside. You have to forgive him. You have to let these bad feelings go. He loved you. You were not just enough, you were everything."

They sat without speaking in the cozy kitchen. A weight lifted from Naomi's heart. Her mother was right. She was old enough to understand. She was a parent. She could not let the hurts of the past keep coloring her actions in the future. Let her father rest in peace.

Lilli got up to put the glasses in the sink. Naomi was lost in thought.

"So, what about Sam?" Lilli wiped her hands on a dishtowel and waited for her daughter to speak.

"Sam made his choice, and it wasn't me, Ema. I won't use a baby to get him to change his mind. I will tell him, but not now. Maybe after the baby is born. I can do this." Naomi rose and hugged her mother. Their foreheads touching, their arms around each other, Naomi vehemently whispered to Lilli, "With you and Jonah. I can do it. I don't need him."

CHAPTER TWENTY

"I don't need her!" Sam threw his headset at Tyrone. "I don't know what you think you know, old man, but I don't need Naomi. I don't need anyone."

"You're gonna need two strong men to pick you up off the floor, *boy*, if you ever call me *old man* again." Tyrone rounded on Sam.

The two were in the old bus on Tyrone's farm just outside of Nashville. They were going over the song list for the upcoming Madison Square Garden concert, and Sam had been quarrelsome and difficult all day. His mood had gone from shit to even worse in the week since Naomi had left him alone in Colorado.

"Are you drinkin' again, Hoss?" Tyrone's voice was soft and conciliatory. "You look like the west end of a horse headed east." He laughed but patted Sam's hand as he spoke.

"Why do you think that? I'm fine. I just want to get the rest of this tour straight so we can be done and I can get back to my ranch." Truth be told, Sam had no desire to ever see his ranch again, or at least not until he could get the image of Naomi in his bed, his pool, his stables out of his mind.

"Why do you want to get back there so bad? Seems like you hightailed it out of there pretty fast after Naomi left."

"I did not hightail it, and I don't want to talk about her and her snotty New York attitude."

"She did not have a snotty attitude, and she was more *small-town* than New York City." Sam knew how much Tyrone liked Naomi. He would not let anyone, even Sam, speak ill of her.

"Well, she sure had to get back there fast. She didn't even take time to say good-bye."

Tyrone's bushy eyebrows flew up quizzically. Sam groaned. He had not meant to share that last bit with Tyrone, but Naomi's hasty retreat had been gnawing at him for a week. He had flown east himself only a day later, stopping in Oklahoma to pick up Tommy and then heading on to Nashville to meet with his record company, before descending on Tyrone.

"I should have known that what appeared to be a genuine affection for me and the band and the music was all a ploy to get us to relax around her and give her some juicy bits for her story." That excuse sounded lame even to Sam. He bent over his guitar again, strumming a few awkward chords.

Tyrone rested a gnarled hand on Sam's shoulder. His voice was full of sadness and reproach. "She wasn't like that, Sam, and you know it. She was half in love with you by the time we played Salt Lake City."

Sam's head whipped up. His eyes were glacial blue and his voice harsh as he snarled back at Tyrone. "She sure didn't act like it in Colorado. She threw this *I love you* at me and then turned tail and left."

Tyrone whistled long and low and stared at Sam. "She told you she loved you? And what did you say?"

"I told her I loved her too." Sam looked away uncomfortably from Tyrone's searching gaze.

"How did you tell her?"

"How do you think I told her? I said it and she just froze up and walked out on me." Sam's eyes were blue ice as he snapped back at Tyrone.

"How *exactly* did you tell her?" Tyrone's eyes narrowed as he watched Sam's face.

"Damn it, I just told you! She said 'I love you, Sam' and I said 'I love you, too, darlin'.'" Sam's back was up with Tyrone's seemingly unrelenting questions.

"You horse's ass! That's what you say to everybody!"

"What do you mean? I don't tell everyone I love them. You *are* getting senile!"

Tyrone rocked back in his chair, shaking his head. A grin was just beginning to play across his wide mouth. "Boy, how do you know so little about yourself?" Tyrone's gnarled hands scrubbed his face in frustration. "Sam, every time a fan or a reporter or a roadie or a promoter or another singer says 'I love you' you say 'I love you too, darlin'. You've been doing it for years. It's like autopilot with you. It's easy, it makes everyone feel good, and you don't have to think about it. If that is what you said to Naomi, no wonder she left. She spills her heart to you—and that couldn't have been easy for her after what she's been through—and you give her your pat reply? You're lucky she didn't slap your face."

"She looked like she wanted to." Realization was slowly dawning on Sam. He knew now that he did love Naomi, the last week of agonizing longing had taught him that. *Why didn't I say the words she wanted to hear?* The last time he said those words was to his dying wife. Saying those words to Naomi in the house where his grief had almost killed him had been beyond him. But the pain he felt at losing Naomi was worse than the pain he felt remembering Beckie. He felt alive with Naomi, for the first time in years, for the first time in maybe forever. *Have I really lost her?*

"What can I do, Ty? How do I make it up to her? I don't want to lose her."

"Well, son, first you better call her. If she won't speak to you, then you are going to have to haul that stupid ass of yours up to New York and convince her. That song you've been noodling with might just do it."

Sam slapped his old friend on the thigh. Looking at his watch, the digital message of the time glowed in the dim light: 09/10/01. 10:00 PM. "It's late there now, she might be asleep. I'll call her in the morning."

CHAPTER TWENTY-ONE

Naomi was not an early riser, but now every morning waves of nausea hit her full force between five and six. She stumbled down the hall from her old bedroom to the bathroom. Fifteen minutes later, after splashing some cold water on her face and a good teeth brushing, she felt human again. She crawled back into bed and slept.

Stretching into wakefulness, her eyes opened slowly. No nausea. Glancing at the clock, she realized she had slept soundly for three more hours. And she was hungry. Up and out of bed, old turquoise moccasins on her feet, she slipped her favorite bathrobe over Winnie-the-Pooh's faded smile and made her way to the kitchen.

"Morning, Ema." She planted a kiss on her mother's cheek on her way to the teapot on the kitchen counter. No coffee for her. Herbal tea was her pregnancy morning drink of choice.

Lilli placed a bowl of oatmeal in front of her daughter. "You look better, *shayna*. How is the nausea? You're not so pale. You look like you did when you came home from college for vacations. Hair in a messy ponytail and I think you had that bathrobe even then." Joining Naomi at the table, she pushed a small pitcher of milk to her daughter.

"Mmmm, this smells so good. You put in brown sugar and raisins, didn't you?"

"Of course. I remember how you like it. You need to eat, you're getting skinny."

"Just like with Jonah, remember? He made me so sick the first three months I ended up weighing less when he was born than I weighed when I got pregnant." Naomi scooped up some oatmeal and smacked her lips in appreciation of the flavors from her youth.

The two women sat in companionable silence for a few moments. It was a pretty morning. Jonah was still asleep. Music played softly in the background. Country music of course, Lilli's favorite. Naomi recognized the strains of "Austin."

"We met Blake Shelton on the tour. He seems like a nice guy." Naomi remarked to her mother.

"Oh, I love his songs! I think he will be a big star." Lilli looked at the clock. "It is almost nine o'clock. Should I wake Jonah or let him sleep?"

"Let him…." Naomi's voice broke off as she heard Sean, the DJ on WGNA break in. "We have a report of a plane flying into the Twin Towers in New York City."

"Oh, that's not funny. Ema, he shouldn't joke about that. A lot of people from this area travel to New York for work and a lot of State employees are in the Twin Towers." Sean could be a bit irreverent and he liked to play pranks on his listeners.

"I don't think he would joke about something like that. Maybe it's a mistake." Lilli shook her head, defending her favorite DJ, when the cohost Ritchie said, as if he heard her, "It must be a mistake. Probably a single engine plane that went off course."

Naomi was already on her feet and rushing for the television in the living room. As she clicked on the remote, she reached for her cellphone. The TV came to life. There was the North Tower, its top engulfed in dark gray smoke, a gaping hole in one side with orange flames dancing along its edges. "Ema!" She shouted as she frantically dialed Jed's number. He finally answered. "Are you okay, Jed? I just heard there's an explosion or something at the Trade Center."

"Yes, I'm fine. Are you still at your mom's? Stay there, we don't know what is happening here. But it was a plane. They say it's a plane. We can see the smoke."

"What is it, Jed? What is happening?"

"Its terrorists, Naomi. I *know* it! It's Goddamned fucking terrorists again. I have to go. We are all fine, we are okay. Stay at your mom's, don't come down here 'til they figure this out. Stay safe."

"You too, Jed, stay safe. Go home. I love you." She said as his phone clicked off. Her mom stood beside her, wringing her hands, muttering in German and Yiddish, staring at the television, listening to the thready voices of Katie Couric and Matt Lauer as they spoke to bystanders, trying to piece the story together.

Hearing the noise, Jonah came wandering into the living room, wiping sleep from his eyes, yawning, as he said, "What is going on? What are you guys watching?" His eyes focused on the screen just as a huge billow of smoke emerged from the second tower. "What the hell? Mom, did you see that? What the hell! Mom, that's the Trade Center!" His astonished eyes searched his mother's face. As Matt Lauer was saying another plane had hit the tower, the producer from NBC he was speaking to interrupted him with, "A DC 9 or 747 just flew by my window and into the tower."

Naomi stared at the horrific sight unfolding before her eyes and the eyes of the world. With one hand, she reached out to grab Jonah tightly to her side. With her other hand she pushed the buttons on her cell, trying to reach Janice, her assistant, who was staying at her loft while Naomi was in Saratoga. *All circuits are busy.* She grabbed her mother's telephone and dialed the loft's number. Janice answered on the first ring. "Oh my God, Naomi. Have you seen the news? Have you seen it? What is happening? Oh, no. Oh, no!"

Naomi said, as calmly as she could, "Janice, I just talked to Jed. Stay in the loft. You will be safe there. Stay in the loft, don't go outside. We are still at my mom's and we're okay. We'll stay here and you stay at my loft. Okay? Just stay there."

"Okay, Naomi, okay. I'll stay. I'm okay. My husband is here with me. But Naomi, those poor people, those poor people in those buildings…" She started to cry.

After calming down Janice, Naomi hung up. Her arm still around Jonah, her free hand stroked her belly. *Poor babies, my poor babies. What kind of world am I bringing this child into? What kind of future will Jonah and Sam's baby have? Sam! Is HE in New York? When was he supposed to come to New York?*

Sam was still asleep in his suite at the Vanderbilt Hotel in Nashville. It had been almost midnight when he returned from Tyrone's spread outside the city. He tossed and turned until just before dawn, thoughts of Naomi splintering his sleep. Groggily, he lifted his head and looked around, trying to get his bearings, trying to figure out where all the noise was coming from. The pounding came from his own damn door. Easing from the tangled sheets, Sam pulled on the crumpled jeans lying in a ball at his feet. Rubbing his hands through his hair in his typical gesture of annoyance, he strode to the door and yanked it open. There stood a red-faced and slightly out of breath Tyrone. He pushed past Sam into the room. Before Sam slammed the door shut, Tyrone clicked on the television. The burning towers filled the screen.

"What the hell is that, Tyrone? What is going on? Good God! Is that New York?"

"Damned straight it is. That is the World Trade Center, boy. Two planes have slammed into it and the damned Pentagon too. We are under attack. I've been trying to call you, but cell phone service sucks. Must be everybody in the world is on the phone right now. Did you call Naomi yet?"

"Naomi! No, Jesus, no. I just woke up, I was up all night. I drifted off around four or five. I don't know. Jesus, where's my phone? Where is the fire? Is it near her apartment or her office? Christ, where is my damn phone?" Sam went back into the bedroom and found his phone on the nightstand. He quickly dialed Naomi's number but could not get through.

"Who can we call? Tommy? Does Tommy have her editor's number? Will he know where she is? Oh, God, poor Jonah. The poor kid must be terrified." Sam started fumbling with his cellphone.

"Don't try to call Tommy with that, Sam. Use the hotel phone. Maybe the land lines are working better than the cells." Tyrone pointed to the phone on the desk, then turned back to the television.

Sam punched in Tommy's home number but got his answering machine. After leaving a terse message, he dialed his manager's office number. Fortunately, Tommy answered on the first ring.

"Tom, it's me, Sam. I need Naomi's numbers. I mean, I need her office number. I need to find out if she is in New York, if she is okay. She's not answering her cell. I...need... I just need..." Sam's voice broke.

"I'll call her office from here, Sam. I'll find out where she is. Just hang in there." In a few moments, Tommy was back on the line. "I can't get through to Rolling Stone, Sam. The lines are jammed; service is not available. I don't know if the lines are down because of these attacks or are just overloaded, but I can't get through to New York City."

Sam slammed the phone down as Tyrone turned to him and said, "Jesus, Sam, there's another plane down. Somewhere in Pennsylvania. Jesus, what is happening?"

Sam paced the room, like a caged leopard. All he could think about was Naomi caught in the city, covered in dirt and debris or burned or lost. Or gone. *No, she couldn't be gone.* He would know it if she was gone. He would sense it somehow. He just had to find her.

"Wait, Tyrone. I know. I have her mother's number on my cell. We used it to call Jonah a few times after the SPAC show. Let me find it." Sam scrolled through numbers, searching for a 518 area code. "I got it. I got it! Naomi would call her mother if she was in New York, she'd call her to let her know she is okay."

"Sam, the lines are down in New York. If Naomi is there, she probably can't get through to anyone."

But Sam was already punching numbers into the phone on his lap. *Answer me, please answer me*, he silently prayed. The phone rang once, then twice. On the third ring, he heard Naomi's voice. "Hello?"

All Naomi heard was a crackling on the line. She was about to hang up when Sam finally spoke, "Naomi? It's Sam. I...saw what was happening in New York and I...ah...I...ah...just wanted to make sure you and Jonah were okay." His voice sounded strained and far away.

"Yes, Sam, we are fine. We've been visiting my mother for a few days. We are all okay. Where are you? Are you in New York?"

"No, the concert we planned for the first of September was postponed, some problems with the sound system. I'm in Nashville. Tyrone..." Sam's voice was gone. Then, Naomi heard Tyrone whispering something to Sam, something like *tell her.*

"Naomi, hello, little girl, it's Tyrone. You all stay up there in the country until this mess settles down, you hear?" Naomi smiled at the gruff affection in the older man's voice. "I'll keep an eye on ole Sam here in Nashville. You know, he was worried sick about you, and he just had to track you down and make sure you all were...."

Once again, more harsh whispers interrupted the call. Then Sam was back on the line. "Well, um, yeah. Tyrone is right. You and Jonah should stay up there in Saratoga until things settle down in New York. I...we...are all real sorry about what happened. Is all your family... I mean...your friends and all in New York...is everyone okay?"

"I checked in with Jed and Janice and they are fine. William is out of the country." Naomi paused as the realization hit her. "Oh, my God. I didn't check on Jonah's father. I didn't call. Damn. Sam, thank you for calling, but I have to call David. Good-bye." Naomi hung up the phone and quickly dialed David's office in Manhattan. Busy. *All circuits are busy.* "Double damn. Now, I'll have to call the house on Long Island. Damn."

Hearing her swear all the way in the kitchen, Jonah came to his mother's rescue. He picked up his grandmother's ancient telephone and punched in the numbers to his father's house. After a few short sentences with the housekeeper, he hung up, smirking at his mom. "Well, Mom, the news is good and bad. Dad and Courtney and the baby are in Connecticut at her brother's house for some family party or something."

"What's the bad news, Jonah?"

He laughed, bitterly. "Dad and his new family are in Connecticut with family. Get it? He's not in New York."

Naomi hugged her son, giving his head a knuckle rub, easing the moment with laughter, silently acknowledging the bitter truth that his father had not called to see if he was okay, if he was safe. "Some things never change, do they, Mom?" Naomi nodded at the truth in Jonah's words. "But, hey, Sam called. He must have gone crazy trying to track you down. How did he sound?"

"He sounded a little crazy." They laughed together. "Yeah, he sounded a little crazy, Jonah. But, it is a crazy day. It is a really crazy, sad, screwed up day, son." Naomi's arms wrapped around Jonah in a fierce hug. "I love you, and I am so grateful you are here with me."

Sam was going crazy. Throwing clothes in his suitcase, throwing questions at Tyrone while he packed.

"I can't fly up there. They've grounded all the planes, I don't know for how long. I am just gonna drive to New York." He looked over at Tyrone who just sat on the bed grinning at him.

"What are you smiling about, old man? This is not funny."

"I don't for a minute think this is funny. I *do* think that it is a damn sad shame that it takes a disaster of this magnitude to shock some sense into you. I am smiling at the vagaries of Fate and at the notion of you driving all the way to New York in a pick-up truck when you don't even know if that little lady will see you. But, hey, I am all for it. Do you want me to come with you?"

"No! I mean, thanks, but no. I have to do this on my own. But, do you have any cash on you? I don't want to go to the bank and who knows if credit cards and ATMs are going to be working or not, especially once I get to New York. Do you think they will restrict other travel?" Both men just stared at each other, the gigantic scope of the day's tragic events sweeping over them. Sam was in turmoil but the country was in even greater turmoil, not knowing if the attacks were over or just beginning.

Tyrone handed Sam a wad of bills. "You know I hate those ATM machines. I always carry a hunk of money around because you never know…" His voice trailed off for a few moments, his eyes flitting over to the awful images on the television screen. "Well, you just never know. But, you should be fine. Just head north up through Kentucky and Ohio. Cut across that little bit of Pennsylvania. You won't be anywhere near where those poor bastards crashed that plane. You'll get to western New York and then you can just drive across Route 90 like we did this summer coming from Syracuse to Albany. It's going to take some time, but you can do it. Cell phones are still messed up and will likely be worse when you get to New York, but they might have it straightened out by tomorrow." Sam stuffed the proffered cash into his jacket pocket and swung his suitcase off the bed. The older man grabbed him in a fierce hug. "You'll be fine. Just don't screw it up with Naomi. Do you know what you're gonna say to her?"

"I have no idea. But I've got a thousand miles to figure it out." Sam moved toward the door of the suite. He stopped and turned. "Ty, thank you. And…" His shoulders stiffened but his chin came up and he looked straight in his old friend's eyes. "I love you. Take care of yourself."

Tyrone's faded eyes filled with tears. "I love you, too, son."

CHAPTER TWENTY-TWO

Naomi was up again the next morning at the crack of dawn. She had not slept well, after watching news reports until almost midnight. Hoping the nausea would not wake her up early, shortly before six, stomach roiling, she gave up on that wish. After her trip to the bathroom, she did not go back to bed. Restless, she wandered into the kitchen and put on the teakettle, knowing some herbal tea would calm her still jittery stomach. While the water heated up, Naomi went to the front door, to bring in the morning papers. The Albany and New York papers sat on the doorstep. As she rose from bending to snatch them up, Naomi spied a huge black pick-up truck parked in her mother's driveway. A pick-up truck sporting Kentucky plates. She could just make out a faded baseball cap on the head of whoever was slumped behind the wheel.

Clutching her ratty pink robe around her, Naomi approached the driver's side and rapped sharply on the window. The baseball cap shot up, on top of a mass of black spiky curls, wary blue eyes, and more than one day's growth of beard. *Sam*! Naomi stepped back as Sam opened the driver's door. His long legs swung down to the paved driveway, his favorite black cowboy boots, scuffed and dusty, planted near her turquoise moccasins.

"Sam! What are you doing here?"

"I was in the area and thought I would check up on you and your mom. And Jonah, too, of course." Sam pulled his Yankees cap off his head and ran his hand through his flattened hair in a gesture so familiar it tore at her heart.

"You were in the area? I thought you were in Nashville yesterday."

"I was, but then I was in New York so I came by."

"To check up on me and my mom?"

"Well, yes, and Jonah. How is he?"

"He's asleep, Sam."

"I thought you would all be asleep so when I pulled in here a little bit ago, I just figured I'd wait in the truck 'til I saw some signs of life." His eyes swept her face. She hoped he would not note the dark circles under her eyes, and the way her robe hung loosely on her frame. She knew she looked tired and thinner and he looked so damn good, she wanted to just wrap her arms around him and never let go. Sam's voice broke into her thoughts. "Wait, what are you doing up so early? You love to sleep in, do you have something going on?"

"No. I didn't sleep well...after yesterday. I just tossed and turned so I decided to get up and make a cup of tea. You might as well come in. I need to turn off the tea kettle. And we don't need to give the neighbors a show, though I doubt anyone is up yet." Naomi turned to go back into the house, but stopped when Sam's hand grasped her shoulder.

"Naomi, before I go inside your mother's house, I need to say something. I can't go in there until I do." She turned slowly to face him, unsure of what was coming next.

"First, I want to apologize for what happened in Colorado." When she started to speak, Sam laid a finger across her lips. "No, let me talk, let me finish. I am sorry for how I reacted when you told me you loved me." Her cheeks flamed at the memory of those humiliating moments. "I could say you caught me off-guard. I could say I was thinking of Beckie. But the truth is, I was scared. I was scared of you loving me and me disappointing you or hurting you. I was so scared I hurt you anyway. And I do apologize."

"I accept your apology, Sam. Now, come inside."

"I'm not finished yet." He took her hands in his. She looked down, afraid to look in his eyes, afraid to see what was in them, even more afraid for him to see what was in her eyes. "Look at me, Naomi. Please, darlin', just look at me." Tears filled her eyes, but she looked up. "Naomi, I love you. I thought it was just lust, and then I thought it was a love affair, but then you walked away from me, and nothing has been right in my life since. I love you. And..." Sam dropped to his knee there in the dew-covered grass on

Iroquois Avenue in Saratoga Springs, on a quiet September day, in a world gone mad, and said, "Will you marry me?"

The tears spilled down Naomi's cheeks, plopping on her robe and on their joined hands. She loved him but she had to tell him her secret before she could accept his proposal. There could only be truth between them from now on, no secrets.

"Sam, get up. I need to tell you something before I can answer your question. If you want to withdraw your proposal after, I won't hold you to it." Confused, Sam rose to his feet, but he still held her hands. "Well, you're not going to believe this—I can hardly believe it myself—but I'm pregnant."

"Pregnant? I thought you were on the pill." She pulled her hands out of his grasp.

"I was on the pill! They just don't work one-hundred percent of the time." Her temper rose. *God damn it.* She knew he would throw it in her face. Like it was her fault! She started to turn away from him, ready to run in the house and slam the door in his face, when she heard his fervent whisper, "Thank God!"

Seconds later Sam crushed Naomi in his embrace. His big body shook with emotion and their tears mingled, as held her and laughed.

"Say yes. Say yes, Naomi. Don't make me beg you." He lifted his head and gazed at her with eyes of brilliant blue.

"Yes. Yes, Sam. I'll marry you. I love you too, darlin'." Sam swatted her tush at the impertinent remark, then lifted her in his arms to carry her back into her mother's house.

EPILOGUE—2016

Fiddling with his onyx cufflinks, Sam walked into the bedroom seeking Naomi's help. She was still standing, looking out the window, wrapped in a towel.

"Naomi, what the hell? Why aren't you dressed?" His voice was harsh in the silence of the room. Startled from her reverie, Naomi turned to him, and he saw then the tears glistening in her eyes.

"What's wrong, darlin'? Are you all right?" Worried, Sam rushed to her side. He was so protective of her. He still could not imagine his life without her. She smiled and hugged him.

"Nothing is wrong, Sam, everything is right. We are *so* lucky. I am so lucky to have you in my life. It's been a great ride."

Sam kissed her. "No, I am so lucky to have you. You are worth more than any award. Do you want to stay home tonight?" His brow was furrowed with worry.

"Absolutely not! I want to see my handsome husband on the stage accepting his lifetime achievement award." Laughing, Naomi broke away from him and headed toward the bathroom to finish dressing.

Two adolescent girls burst in the room then, amidst giggles and tumbling words, wearing nearly identical dresses, the blonde one in black and the brunette in white. Identical twins except for hair color, Naomi insisted they need not be identical in any other way. She had no worries on that account. Inseparable, they played off each other but maintained their own images and interests. Rachel was the sweetie, in love with her father, her mother, her brother, her sister, and the world. She was a dreamer, an artist and musician. Leah was all business. She was curious about everything, from the farm equipment to the mechanics of writing a good song or a good story. And she was a terrible tease, like her Aunt Miriam, but without a malicious bone in her body. Let anyone try to come between the girls and they became a single immovable object. Naomi was so glad her two daughters were friends as well as siblings. No rivalry existed there, no one-upsmanship like the troubled relationship she had shared with Miriam. But her girls were loved equally by both their parents, parents who loved them for who they were. In this, at least, Sam and Naomi shared perfect agreement.

Religion was another matter that had not divided them. The girls were Jewish, like Jonah, and Sam had become a willing participant in Sunday School and the Jewish holidays. The ranch sparkled with lights for the whole month of December in celebration of Hanukkah and Christmas. Whether Rachel Sarah and Leah Rebecca would attend summer camp or go on tour had not been as easily resolved. Nor had the fate of the horses Sam had given them for their last birthday. "Why not ponies?" Naomi fumed at him. "Little ponies!" They were as daring on horseback as their father had been, much to Naomi's consternation and Sam's delight.

Rachel, in black, danced over to her father, while Leah headed straight for the jewelry on the dresser.

"Ema, why aren't you wearing your necklace? Can I wear it?" Leah, the girly-girl of the two, pleaded, lifting the heavy necklace.

Naomi walked out, sheathed in sparking black lace from shoulder to ankle. "No, you may not. Rubies and pearls are not for young ladies!" She slipped the bracelet on her wrist and turned to Sam as she fastened the necklace around her neck. The necklace he gave her when the song he wrote about her and their tumultuous summer together—"Rubies and Pearls"—became his biggest hit. Sam sat on the bed, balancing Rachel on his lap while she straightened his tie. Her husband, their girls, love and laughter. It was everything to Naomi, almost everything. Jonah's laughing emergence from the hall finished the family scene and made her world complete.

"You all are *so* late!" Her tall, handsome son said, scooping Leah into his arms. "The limo driver just called up and said we have to be downstairs *and* in the car in fifteen minutes or we are going to miss the opening." He laughed, her father's laugh, but secure and happy. Reminded of the mad dash to the limo all those years ago in Philadelphia, in the days when her only prayer was for her son's happiness, Naomi smiled. Jonah was a lawyer now, recently admitted to the New York State Bar. He worked in the Manhattan District Attorney's Office and lived in the loft that had been his childhood home with Naomi. She and Sam and the girls spent most of their time on a ranch in Oklahoma, the Colorado mountain retreat or their newly-purchased horse farm in Saratoga.

With a quick glance at their watches, Sam and Rachel trooped out behind Jonah and Leah. Naomi grabbed her wrap. She paused before she turned out the lights, and, smiling, looked at the glittering Manhattan skyline once again. *Sometimes* prayers are *answered and the answer is* yes.

THE END

YIDDISH GLOSSARY

Bubbe: Grandmother
Bubele: Darling (usually applied to children)
Ema: Mother
Essen: Eat
Gehenom: Hell
Ketzela: Kitten, an endearment
Kokhlefl: Pot-stirrer, meddler, a person who stirs up trouble
Megilah: A long involved story
Mishegas: Craziness
Mezuzah: A small, cylindrical container with a rolled Hebrew script inside containing a portion of Deuteronomy, hand-written on parchment. Mounted on doorframe.
Oy: Interjection of pain, weariness, disgust, resignation, or surprise
Plotz: To faint, flop down, expire from excitement
Putz: Stupid, ignorant person (vulgar: penis)
Schlep: Pull, drag
Schmuck: Jerk, fool, idiot
Shabbes: Sabbath, from sundown Friday to sundown Saturday
Shayna punim: Pretty face
Shiksa: Non-Jewish girl, derogatory
Tush: Butt, bottom, derriere
Vilde Chaya: Wild person (literally, wild animal)
Zissen Nishumele: Sweet soul

ABOUT MORGAN MALONE

Morgan Malone has been reading romance since the age of twelve when she snuck her mother's copy of *Gone with the Wind* under the bed covers to read by flashlight. A published author at the age of eight, she has been writing romance for the last six years, after retiring from a thirty-year career as a judge and counsel at a small New York State agency. Morgan lives near Saratoga Springs, NY, with her chocolate Labrador Retriever. When not writing erotic romance, Morgan can be found penning her memoirs or painting watercolors.

Visit her on Facebook
https://www.facebook.com/morgan.malone.39
or her at Website
http://www.morganmaloneauthor.com/

ALSO AVAILABLE BY MORGAN MALONE

Out of Control

Cocktales

If you enjoyed Morgan Malone's *Unanswered Prayers,* please consider telling others and writing a review on Amazon or GoodReads.

.

70177000R00092

Made in the USA
Columbia, SC
01 May 2017